THE AMERICAN WEST
COWBOYS

Grayson Wyatt

Copyright © 2016 by Grayson Wyatt. All rights reserved. No part of this book may be reproduced, stored in a retrieval system, or transmitted in any form or by any means, electronic, mechanical, photocopying, recording, scanning, or otherwise except as permitted under Section 107 or 108 of the 1976 United States Copyright Act, without either the prior written permission of New Word City. Requests for permission should be addressed to the **editors@newwordcity.com**. For more information about New Word City, visit our Web site at **www.newwordcity.com**

1
THE COWBOYS   5
2
THE CATTLE BARONS   29
3
A COWBOY'S LIFE   57
4
THE ROUNDUP   77
5
THE LONG DRIVE   99
6
COW TOWNS   139
EPILOGUE   165
SOURCES   169

1
THE COWBOYS
"HE STAYED WITH THE HERD"

The land was out there, past the rolling muddy waters of the Mississippi River and the states that hugged its banks. In the years after the Civil War, as the nation tried to heal itself, this land to the west must have seemed nearly another country, a different place altogether.

It was a harsh land, an enormous plain that stretched across a third of the continental United States to the Rocky Mountains that guarded the country's final third. The land was filled with extremes: bitterly cold winters, brutal summer heat, barren deserts, and lush valleys with meadows and tree-lined streams. The ground was clay and sand and pebbles, deposited by the wild rivers that raced down from the Rockies. To the west of an invisible boundary that ran through the Dakotas and down into Texas, rainfall averaged less than twenty inches a year. And much of that never got a chance to soak in. The wind - a howling presence that never ceased - made sure of that. It was no place for a farmer, no place for a plow.

Across this expanse were only a handful of towns with populations of more than 5,000.

The East was already stitched together by rail lines, bringing prosperity by the carload behind smoke-belching engines. But west of Missouri, only a single railroad ran toward the Pacific nearly 2,000 miles away. The golden spike linking East and West on the Union Pacific Railroad was driven in 1869 in what was still Utah Territory, and this lifeline was still tenuous. Some days, only a single train ran over the rickety rail bed.

Geographers and explorers dismissed this land. They called it the Great American Desert. Not just for its lack of rain – that was a given – but more because it was perceived as a place to get through on the way to somewhere better.

It wasn't that people hadn't tried to figure out how to make a life on the Great Plains. Even before the Civil War, schemers and dreamers had gone in search of riches – only to end up shaking their heads in disappointment. They had found little that would make them want to recommend the land to others.

Francis Parkman, a Boston historian who crossed the plains in 1846, wrote of the bleakness: "No living thing was moving through the vast landscape, except the lizards that darted over the sand and through the rank grass and prickly pears at our feet. . . . Before and behind us, the level monotony of the plain was unbroken as far as the eye could reach. Sometimes it glared in the sun, an expanse of hot, bare sand; sometimes it was veiled by coarse grass. Skulls and whitening bones of buffalo were scattered everywhere."

The lack of water meant that corn or wheat wouldn't grow here, but Parkman and others dismissed the asset right in front of them.

It was grass.

Across the semi-arid plains was a blanket of grasses, principally gama and buffalo grass. These grasses could withstand drought; buffalo grass needed less than fifteen inches of annual rain. Dried under a baking sun, the grass cured on the ground into a hay-like feed that provided nourishment even in the winter.

The grasses had once supported the buffalo. Great herds of the beasts had roamed the plains - by some estimates, nearly 75 million across the nation's midsection. But that age was all but over as a systematic hunt, fueled by demand for buffalo hides, reduced the thundering herds to an afterthought. The grass kept growing, of course, waiting for another creature that could survive on the range.

That animal would be the longhorn. It was an ornery creature, descended from cattle brought to the New World by the Spaniards. After three centuries of surviving the heat, cold, lack of water, and fierce predators of the Great Plains, the longhorn was rangy, lean, and tough. It could live in the cruel climate of the American West.

But that wasn't all. There was now money to be made in bringing the cattle from the Great American Desert to the railheads in Iowa and Kansas and Missouri that tied into the big cities in the East. It was a migration no less extraordinary than the wanderings of the buffalo. But this time it was controlled by men, who in the two decades between 1867 and 1887 drove some 5.5 million cows out of the southern Plains. In turn, they set in motion a chain of events that created a new West in a forbidding region that had been long regarded as worthless.

These men weren't just any men. They were as tough as the cattle they drove. They worked hard. They played harder. They were cowboys.

In the popular culture and the eyes of the world, the cowboy is the quintessential American. Cowboys were tough, resourceful, hard-working, and self-reliant. On the lawless frontier, they lived by their own Code of the West – and enforced it with their six-shooters. They faced down rustlers, desperadoes, wolves, mountain lions, rattlesnakes, and fierce Indian warriors. They drove millions of cattle for thousands of miles along rough trails, through blizzards and hailstorms, across deserts and raging rivers, to get to wide-open railhead towns, where they went wild on drunken sprees. Cowboys were generous, free-spending, naïve, and impetuous. Their code permitted violence, cruelty, and vigilante justice.

But they were honorable men: Their word was their bond, dependable as the seasons. They never deserted their posts or let down a friend. They revered a virtuous woman.

Of course, all this is largely a myth. Even at the height of the cowboy era, the word itself had various meanings; on the southwestern frontier in Arizona, "cowboy" signified a rustler and outlaw with hardly any redeeming qualities. But the cowboy legend was born in reality - and escalated rapidly in newspaper reports and the dime novels of the late nineteenth century. Then the myth was embellished and perpetuated in touring Wild West shows well into the twentieth century. And it finally reached its zenith in Hollywood's classic Western movies: *Stagecoach, High Noon, The Treasure of the Sierra Madre, True Grit, Lonesome Dove.* Name your favorite.

But we are stuck with the portrayal for better or worse.

Cowboys are such a huge part of the American identity and culture that it's easy to assume that their way of life endured for generations.

It didn't.

While the job started evolving in the 1830s and vestiges of it linger still in the West, the heyday of the cowboy was brief - perhaps twenty years after the Civil War.

What were cowboys really like? While there were grizzled hands among them, most cowboys were young men; their average age was twenty-four. They had grit, gumption, and more than occasional naiveté; they were minimally educated, with a shrugging disdain for "book-learning," and knew hardly anything of the world outside their small communities. During the era of the cowboy, perhaps 40,000 men worked the great herds of cattle on the Western range and on their journeys to market.

But the numbers don't tell the whole story. Statistics can't always measure influence. If the cowboys hadn't existed, we might have had to invent them. They spoke to American ideals and the tradeoff between community and individualism.

William H. Forbis wrote in his book, *Cowboys*:

"They were men of a particular time and place, living by a code compounded of hard-fisted frontier desperation and Victorian-era social values, performing body-punishing and hazardous jobs, and pitting themselves against a land of sweeping grandeur that offered prodigious drafts of misery."

Consider the diary of George Duffield, who set out from Iowa in 1866 to drive cattle from Texas back north to his home. (Duffield is said to be the inspiration for the character Gil Favor on the television series *Rawhide*, which was broadcast from 1959 to the mid-1960s.) His entries paint a vivid portrait of the mental and physical toil that cowboys endured: "June 12: Hard Rain & Wind. Big stampede & here we are among the Indians with 150 head of Cattle gone. Hunted all day & the Rain pouring down with but poor success. Dark days are these to me. Nothing but Bread & Coffee. Hands all Growling & Swearing - everything wet & cold. Beeves gone . . . rode all day & gathered all but 35. Mixed with 8 other Herds Last Night 5000 Beeves stampeded at this place & a general mix up was the result."

Two days later, he wrote: "We are now 25 miles from Ark River & it is Very High we are water bound by two creeks & but Beef & Flour to eat, am not Homesick but Heart sick."

Beyond recording the storms and the stampedes, Duffield's diary opens a window into something larger than the journey itself. There were beautiful valleys and the pleasures found in sweet blackberries and of freshly caught fish. There were skirmishes with Indians - and blistered backs and hands. The river crossings were dangerous. Duffield was attacked coaxing a beeve (a common name for cattle derived from the word beef) across a stream. He nearly drowned. At one point, he says simply, "Have not got the Blues but am in Hel of a fix."

Even so, the life grabbed him.

But it wasn't only farmhands from Iowa who caught the cowboy fever. John Baumann, an Englishman, came to Texas to become a frontiersman and get rich. He quickly found himself in an environment of consequence. His job was to round up a herd of horses that had become sick through eating a toxic plant called locoweed. The horses were reeling, groaning on the ground, and foaming at the mouth. Some were already dead. Baumann and the others had to move the animals to a ranch 180 miles away, across the prairie. For three weeks, they made the sad march, with the herd thinning out each day like seed corn trickling out of a torn burlap bag. In his words: "Every morning in the chill half-light of early dawn, it was our sad duty to lift those who had lain down to rest, and, by rubbing their stiffened, trembling limbs, to restore circulation sufficiently to enable them to stand. Others were beyond help, and several times, I have given such their quietus with a six-shooter bullet without drawing more than a faint trickle of blood, so poor were they."

Even the respites offered heartbreak. J. L. McCaleb was a boy when he rode up the old Chisholm Trail from Texas to Kansas with a herd of longhorns from Texas. One night, he got permission to go to a saloon and dance hall. He recalled that it had been a while since he had seen either a building or a woman, and they both looked pleasing. McCaleb wrote in his journal: "I went to the bar and called for a toddy, and as I was drinking it, a girl came up and put her little hand under my chin, and looked me square in the face and said, 'Oh, you pretty Texas boy, give me a drink.' I had a five-dollar bill, so I told that girl that she could make herself easy; that I was going to break the monte game, buy out the saloon, and keep her to run it for me when I went back to Texas for my other herd of cattle. Well, I went to the dealer, put my five on the first card, and won. I now had ten dollars, so I put the two bills on the tray and won. Had now twenty dollars and went to get a drink – another toddy - but my girl was gone. I went back and soon lost all I had won and my original five. . . . I went out, found my partner, and left for camp. The next morning, in place of owning the saloon and going back to Texas after my other herd, I felt – 'oh! What's the use?'"

There was humor and tragedy, heartbreak and compassion in the Old West. In many ways, the whole human condition was set loose upon the trails and open prairies that defined the life of a cowboy.

In that largely lawless land, the cowboys developed their own rules of conduct. These rules sprang from a simple sense of fair play, beginning with a man's word – the need to keep a promise. Whole herds were bought and sold on a handshake, and the deal was honored even if a man went bankrupt paying his debt. Once hired, a cowboy "stayed with the herd," no matter how exhausted, cold, hungry, or sick he might be.

Case in point: Early one spring, trailing a herd from New Mexico to Amarillo in the Texas Panhandle, a bunch of cowboys had spent ten days in freezing rain and snow. Then they ran into a dry wind storm from the north with blowing sand that stung their faces and any exposed skin. A hand named George was coughing and shivering. Another cowboy, Mack MacAvoy, urged him to go to his bedroll; the cattle would be safe, he said. But George refused and stayed in the saddle until he toppled off, literally frozen. His buddies buried him on the highest hill they could find. The grave was marked only with a stick of wood, long since rotted. But to those who know the story, said cowboy historian J. Frank Dobie, there is a granite marker there in spirit that reads: "He stayed with the herd."

The cowboys were a mixed lot. Some came from the East, former Union soldiers who had seen war and still craved excitement. There were more former rebel soldiers from the South, men with little desire to stay in their still-ruined section of the country but with lingering loyalty to the Lost Cause.

Some cowboys had spent a previous life at sea. Others came from Europe, both moneyed and penniless immigrants. Some of the Englishmen were known as remittance men, the offspring of England's top families who had been disinherited. College degrees were rare, however. A different education was what counted on the range. As one Texas cowboy said, "Well, when I got so I could draw a cow and mark a few brands on a slate, I figured I was getting too smart to stay in school."

Other cowboys had been drifters and beggars and bums. Some had had run-ins with the law. All of them were intensely private, but generous with food and tobacco. Strangers were invited to share meals and stories, but usually not the details of their lives. That was considered too personal, too probing.

One cowboy recalled an incident when a man rode up to his boyhood home just as the food was being served: "We ate dinner and then I joined my older brother in asking the stranger what his name was. 'Jones is the name,' he said. As soon as he rode off, our mother laid us boys out for being so ill-mannered as to ask any man his name."

What bound these diverse men together was the job at hand, which involved tending the West's endless herds of cattle and moving them from range to buyer. After all, it was a business. A cow that couldn't get to market wasn't worth much. And on the range and the trail, it was the cattle whose welfare took priority. The cowboys were expected to look out for themselves – but only after the animals were taken care of.

While the term cowboy now means something unique, its history is a little uncertain.

During the Revolutionary War, cowboy was the name given to Tories who tinkled cowbells in the fields to lure farmer-patriots into the open. Later, during the Texas independence movement, it referred to bandits who stole cattle from the Mexicans, often at the barrel of a gun. It was only after the Civil War that "cowboy" became the accepted label for the grueling and often exasperating job of tending cattle under the expansive sky of the Great Plains.

In the earliest days, a Texas cowboy might wear an old army uniform and marching boots. The Stetson, with its high crown and wide brim, was not yet prevalent. Instead, the hats were floppier, with a brim that whipped or plastered to the head in the ever-present wind. Barbed wire hadn't yet fenced off and tamed the open range, and cowboys drove the longhorns hundreds of miles across the scrub and prairie. During downtimes, there were other chores: chasing strays, finding wood, hunting wolves.

The roundup and trail work was seasonal, peaking in the summer and slowing to a standstill during the harsh plains winters. During those off months, cowboys might be found in town, bunking with friends and doing odd jobs just to keep busy - and get a little spending money. (The average cowboy spent about seven years on the range before calling it quits and settling down in a frontier town or on a small ranch of his own.)

The cowboys' work revolved around two large mammals. There was the horse, of course. And then there were the beeves: enormous half-ton beasts that took their cues from the instincts of the herd and, if spooked, could run riot at a moment's notice.

The horse was simply a tool for the cowboy. The range was too large and the distances too great for a man on foot. Without a horse, there was no way to round up, brand and move all those cows to market. Most often, the horses were supplied by the ranch. A cowboy who did own his own horse offered it as part of the remuda, or pool of available rides - a gesture of good faith. Like all tools, the horse was taken care of - up to a point. The animals were fed and worked hard, sometimes to their death on particularly grueling long trail drives.

The coldness of this relationship, one based mainly on utility rather than affection, shouldn't detract from another aspect of the intertwining of the cowboy and the horse. The horse became a major part of the cowboy's self-image. Other people - the swells in the city, for example - walked. Cowboys rode. They were tall in the saddle.

Indeed, a good deal of the Code of the West concerned horses. No cowboy borrowed a horse from another man's string without permission (which was rarely given). When two mounted cowboys met each other on a trail, it was good form to keep course and pass a friendly word; to ride off the trail indicated furtiveness or even danger. But neither man should wave, which might scare the other's horse. If one of the two cowboys got off his horse, the other dismounted too, so that they met on equal terms. But a man on foot should never touch the bridle of a ridden horse, since that was seen as interfering with the rider's control of his mount.

In general, to be afoot was to be no man at all, and certainly not a cowboy. James Benton, in his history of cowboys, quotes a former cowpuncher named Jo Mora who noted somewhat wryly that if you took a cowboy off his horse, what you found was "just a plain bowlegged human who smelled very horsey at times, slept in his underwear, and was subject to boils and dyspepsia."

Of course, being a cowboy involved more than just the horse. It was a job as well as a way of life, and it required different tools and the fierce knowledge to use them correctly and quickly. On their saddle, cowboys carried a lariat, a length of rope or braided rawhide that was the multipurpose tool of its day. Looped at one end, it could be thrown to snare a steer's horns or hooves and then looped around the pommel of a saddle, enabling a scrawny man on a horse to control a dangerous animal. It could be joined with other ropes to make a small corral or used as a hobble to keep a horse from wandering too far at night. It was a tow chain for wood or for dragging animals out of water and mud. It was even a kind of talisman: A new rope placed around a sleeping man protected him from snakes, which wouldn't crawl over the bristly fibers jutting from the rope's surface. And on the occasional times that quick justice needed to be dispensed, the lariat was refashioned into a noose.

Equally important, less as a tool than as a statement, was the gun. Ever since the Texas Rangers placed the first major order for Colt revolvers in the late 1840s, the six-gun had been a staple of the Western range.

Rifles were used for hunting but could be a problem on horseback. They were hard to hold with one hand and to stow securely in a scabbard on the saddle. The revolver lacked accuracy, but it was more versatile. There were rattlesnakes to kill, horses with broken legs that needed to be put down, and stampedes that had to be stopped before they careened out of control.

Most of all, shooting guns was fun. Cowboys on the range liked to blaze away at rabbits, snakes, trees, and fence posts; to celebrate being in town on a spree, they liked to shoot wildly into the air. But actual gunfights were far less frequent than the Hollywood Westerns would have us believe.

Just as they understood the power of being on horseback, cowboys also were aware that guns oozed might and manliness. They might weigh themselves down with weaponry whenever they paid a call on a girl, confident that she would be impressed.

But it wasn't just guns that made the man. Cowboys could be real dandies in their own way. A pair of boots, or a fine hat with a fancy sweat band, might set a cowboy back four months' wages. Eventually, the threadbare army uniforms of the early cowboys gave way to jeans, sometimes with leggings called chaps to deflect cactus and spiny brush. At the same time, boots made for walking were traded in for riding boots, with narrow pointed toes. More than fashion was at play here: The pointed toes helped a boot slip out of the stirrup if a rider was thrown. This was important, because the most common cause of death for cowboys was getting dragged by their horses.

It is perhaps not surprising that cowboys looked down - both physically and otherwise - on other folks. They were highly conscious of their special status, and bent every effort to reinforce the tough, all-competent, hard-playing cowboy image. A New Yorker traveling across the plains reported: "There is no use trying to be overbearing with them, for they will not stand the least assumption of superiority."

While they may have had big egos in common, cowboys were quite a diverse bunch. By some estimates, about one cowboy in six or seven was Mexican. A similar number were black, often former slaves from Texas ranches emancipated after the war. There were cowboys with Indian blood. But the majority were white men, and many if not most of them were unabashed in their racism. Blacks and Mexicans routinely were the targets of racial epithets, and on occasion, physical abuse followed the verbal assaults.

Beneath the surface in most cowboys ran a deep streak of stoicism. It wasn't that the job lacked conditions or situations worthy of complaint. Just think about it: On any given day, a cowboy could find himself up against a prairie fire, quicksand, a hailstorm, or a stampede. The work was nearly endless, often eighteen hours a day for seven days a week. Rest was a stinking bedroll. So there was more than enough to moan about. But complaining was what other people did. It was unbecoming a cowboy, unless he could make a joke of it or confide it to a diary.

There was no sympathy or empathy out on the range. The Englishman John Baumann told of a cowhand who rode off one morning to do some hunting. A distant gunshot was heard, and a while later, the cowboy returned to camp. He sat down and began to whittle a stick. Satisfied with the results, he put a rag around the stick and jammed it into a bullet wound in his thigh to stem the bleeding. He then rode off, to find a surgeon some thirty miles away.

Baumann later wrote of the cowboy ethos: "He is in the main a loyal, long-enduring, hard-working fellow grit to the backbone, and tough as whipcord; performing his arduous and often dangerous duties, and living his comfortless life, without a word of complaint about the many privations he has to undergo."

The suffering was in a sense part of the package. When mentioned, the hardships were more likely to be alluded to with a grim wink. After a bitter winter, which killed off cattle by the thousands, gave way to furnace-like heat, a cowhand was observed addressing the sun with the words, "Where the hell was you last January?"

Jokes about the weather underscored a more unsettling fact: It could be a cowboy killer. After riding accidents, pneumonia was the leading cause of death among cowboys.

The tight humor about the hardships went hand in hand with the cowboys' aloofness. Most had a deep disdain for finding comfort or conversation with others. Other than swearing, which at some ranches was ground for dismissal, cowboys were men of few words. Many meals were consumed in silence. Big talkers were frowned upon. Even yarns told around the fire at night were sparse; when they were shared, they were usually brief.

Paradoxically, this laconic composure occasionally gave way to bragging about who was the better cowboy. They not only bragged about themselves but also about others who were even better at their jobs, near-legendary cowboys like Ed Lemmon. By his own estimate, Lemmon drove more than a million head of cattle in his lifetime. On a single day, it was said, he culled and branded 900 cows.

Such exploits swelled into tall tales. There was the Arizona rancher who once boasted that he had riders who could calmly roll and light a cigarette while busting wildly bucking mustangs – a feat, he told a friend, that made the horse realize the hopelessness of bucking any more. His friend, from Montana, bragged back that his riders did the same - except that what the horse saw when he looked back was the cowboy, "quietly shaving, holding a small mirror in one hand and the [straight] razor in the other, with the mug, hot water, and bay rum in a little basket under his arm."

If cowboys had an object of reverence, it was women. This was the Victorian era, after all. But for many of these men, interactions with the opposite sex were few and far between. Their transient life discouraged settling down, and their pay wasn't enough to support a family. The occasional quick visit to a prostitute didn't quell the desire to associate with a woman of virtue. A cowboy would travel miles, by one account, "just to sit on a porch for an hour or two and watch some homesteader's red-faced daughter rock her chair and scratch her elbows – and not a smack or a hug." *The Denver Republican* applauded: "Let a cowboy be alone in the presence of a good woman, and there is no finer gentleman produced by nature."

It's not hard in all these descriptions to find the cowboy essence. It was a violent life of toil, of dark humor, and of understatement about the enormity of the job at hand. As one cowboy, writing to a ranch owner back East, summarized his past year:

Dear sur,

We have brand 800 caves this roundup. We have made sum hay potatoes in a fare crop. That Inglishman you lef in charge at the other camp got to fresh and we had to kill the son of a bitch. Nothing much has happened sense yu lef.

Yurs truly, Jim.

2
THE CATTLE BARONS
"CASTLES ON THE PRAIRIE"

The cowboys were front and center - the stars, in other words, in the saga of the Wild West. But it was the ranch owners who made it all possible, and created huge fortunes in the process.

Like Charles Goodnight.

The year was 1876, and the trail riders and a herd of 1,600 cows were pushing through the Texas Panhandle. Suddenly, the riders saw a break in the unyielding terrain. They found themselves at the lip of a gorge, the Palo Duro Canyon, where the headwaters of the Red River had carved a fertile slice right through the heart of the land.

Among those looking down into the canyon was Goodnight. He was already a legendary rancher and cattle driver, with the bowlegs to prove that he did more than give orders from the comfort of his porch. Big as a steer himself, he was not a man to be trifled with.

Goodnight had made - and then lost - a fortune in the cattle business. His eyes were wide open, and what he saw in the valley with its sheltered pastures and natural fences was a cowboy's paradise. And on that day, he made a decision: By any means necessary, Palo Duro - "Hard Stick" in Spanish - would be his. He would drive out the buffalo that still roamed the canyon floor and the Comanches who camped there. It would take more than grit; it would take money. Goodnight set out to find investors to stake his dream.

Five years later, Goodnight ruled over a fiefdom centered on Palo Duro, but stretching out over the plains. His herd exceeded 100,000 head, and his annual sales brought in $500,000, the equivalent of perhaps $12 million in today's money.

Although his tale was more dramatic than most, Goodnight was just one of the many cattle barons who remade the West. They were men of guts and bull-headed ambition. If you had asked them why they were there, they would have told you it wasn't about the riding, roping, or drama of the cattle drive.

No, it was more basic than that.

Ranching was, for Goodnight and his fellow cattlemen, first and foremost about money. And through these men, the world of the cowboy became intertwined with the world of commerce. The force behind the cattle drives and roundups were investors who helped ranchers stake dubious claims to public lands and, above all, to acquire and sell cattle.

By the mid-1880s, the beginning of the end of the true cowboy era, cattle had become the largest business in the West. At the top of this enterprise was an oligarchy of a few dozen ranch owners who controlled more than 20 million acres of land. Many of these men had been wealthy to start with or were staked by well-heeled investors.

But the door to being a cattle baron wasn't determined solely by birth. Far from being permanently fastened shut, it often just needed a good shove. Some of the barons had started small, working the Texas plains in the years after the state's independence from Mexico in 1836. There were refugees from the East and South, escaping the monotonous toil of the mill and field.

In those early years, it was easy for an enterprising man to hire a few hands and start rounding up wild cattle. Some of the animals were unbranded strays, known as mavericks after a rancher named Sam Maverick, who, for some reason - most likely that he wanted to claim unbranded cattle as his own - never branded his cows.

Other cattle had brands that a well-placed iron could alter. The Code of the West was just developing, and it was oddly flexible when it came to the ownership of cattle. Stealing a horse was one thing – strictly forbidden, punishable by swift death on occasion, since a man without a horse could die on the prairie. But when it came to rustling cattle, it depended largely on who did it, and how.

In those early years, anyone could slap his brand on a maverick regardless of where he found it. Later, it came to be accepted that most mavericks belonged to the owner of the range where they were found. But even then, actual ownership was such a tangle of conflicting claims that cattlemen continued to slap their brands on any unmarked beeves they came across.

Most brands were applied with fixed irons that seared the entire insignia – a double V, for example, or the outline of a crescent moon – into the cow's haunch. But a running iron, a straight iron with a slightly curved tip, could be used to change the brand on an animal with a few quick strokes. A double V could become a double diamond, the same way a failing student might use a pen to make the "F" on his grade report look like a "B." That was outright rustling, but even such tricks might be tolerated by friendly neighboring cattle barons if done sparingly. (They could even joke about it. One cattleman, entertaining a neighbor for dinner, cracked that he was serving "something you've never eaten before – your own beef.")

Similarly, an ambitious ranch foreman who hoped to start his own herd might register a brand and apply it to the mavericks he found on his boss's land, keeping the stolen cattle in secluded river thickets. When George Clutts, a veteran cowboy, asked Charlie Goodnight for a job, Goodnight challenged him: "George, they say you're a cow thief." Clutts retorted, "They say the same thing about you, Mr. Goodnight." Impressed by his brashness, Goodnight hired him then and there.

But a stranger caught trying the same tactics risked summary punishment. Some were actually shot in the act; others were hanged by vigilantes. In 1875, a group of ranchers in Mason County, Texas, broke into a jail to seize five accused cattle rustlers. They executed three of them before the sheriff arrived to rescue the other two.

That was the beginning of the notorious Mason County range war, which lasted for two years and resulted in at least twenty-four deaths. Like other Texas feuds, it was an extension of the American Civil War: The ranchers were German immigrants, loyal to the Union, while the alleged rustlers and their allies, who were homesteaders and small ranchers, were Texans and Confederate sympathizers.

Clearly, the Code of the West included a credo that

might often made right. That extended to the basic business of ownership of the land.

Across the range, the cattle barons were creating empires from little more than pen and paper. The trick was to claim a piece of land as legally one's own. It didn't much matter whether that was true; the claim was enough. For example, this notice appeared in a Montana newspaper in the 1880s: "I, the undersigned, do hereby notify the public that I claim the valley branching off the Glendive Creek, four miles east of the Allard and extending to its source on the south side of the Northern Pacific Railroad as a stock range. Chas. S. Johnson."

In the 1870s and 1880s, as the cattle business boomed and busted, newspapers in the West were stuffed with such ads. Although they read like legal notices, the ads had no legal standing. But they worked, particularly at first, because the claimers were usually powerful men - and the government was too distant to call their bluff.

There was usually a shred of truth to the claim. A cattleman might purchase a homestead - typically 160 acres, or a quarter of a square mile - and then use that as a springboard to claim all that lay beyond, often to the ridge that separated his property from the cattleman trying the same trick on the other side. Even Theodore Roosevelt, fifteen years before he became president, used this tactic in the Dakotas; both his Maltese Cross and Elkhorn

Ranch buildings were on the public domain. But in later years, when the ranchers began fencing their ranges and closing off watering spots, the welter of conflicting claims led to fence-cutting and sometimes outright range wars.

In the free-swinging early days of the range, however, if a shoe-string cattleman got lucky and went to market when prices were high, the payoff fueled further expansion. By claim or by force, he appropriated the grazing land and watering holes that his added cattle demanded. Beyond that, growth required the skills of management and marketing and of finding additional capital to keep growing.

Many of the animals that comprised these original herds were nearly feral, left behind in a previous generation by Mexicans. These wild cows and their offspring roamed the thickets like oversized deer and were said to number in the hundreds of thousands by the end of the Civil War.

By 1860, there were some 3.5 million head of cattle in Texas, and the makings of a business were beginning to develop. But then came the Civil War. Ranchers and cowboys went off to fight for the Confederacy, and their stock was left alone to wander in the Great American Desert. When ranchers resumed business after the war, both the cows and the demand had multiplied.

Although Texas is enormous, the cattle business over time grew too big for a single state. Now, as ranchers moved up the Great Plains, the operations began changing, taking advantage of geography and technology. For one, the distance to the railheads was shorter, so ranches took on a more permanent flavor. The work was more stable, and employees were hired for terms that ran longer than the seasons. In the summer, they cut hay. In the winter, they kept the herds from freezing in blizzards. And all the time, they did what they could to keep the cattle fat. Weight was money.

Over time, these operations grew to encompass tens of thousands of beeves on hundreds of thousands of acres. With numbers that big, decisions were complex and potentially risky.

Consider the dilemma that faced John Clay, the manager of the sprawling V V V Ranch in South Dakota in 1878. The weather had been fine, and the cattle were getting fat on the nutrient-rich grasses of the upper prairie. Prices were high, and Clay decided to wait a few weeks to let them gain even more weight before sending his stock east. During the delay, however, prices on the Midwest exchanges dropped, costing Clay $10,000 (the equivalent of about $230,000 today).

But when the prices held, the cattle business paid off handsomely, making the arduous work profitable for the cattle bosses and their investors.

James Haft and a partner bought 1,000 head of cattle for just under $16,000 in 1881 in what was then the Washington Territory on the Pacific Coast. First, they had to move the cattle east, to the Dakotas. The drive took six months across the Rockies and the Northern Plains, and cost the partners precious cattle. The herd, now down to 900, arrived in late October, just in time for a harsh winter during which temperatures plunged to nearly 40 below. Haft's ears, nose and fingers were frostbitten. But the herd survived, and by the next year, he had nearly 1,500 head, including calves. Haft took 271 cattle to Chicago, made a profit of $10,656, and still had some 1,200 head left.

Despite the dollars and need to profit, the ranching business was built – at least in the beginning – on trust. Deals, early on, were all done on a handshake. The cowboys who delivered the cattle were given a bill of sale from the owner of the herd. That paper transferred to the shipper, and finally to the slaughterhouse - and then the money moved in the other direction. But over time, a more complex system of factoring, loans, and promissory notes came to the fore. Credit - and how to get it on the best possible terms - became as great a concern as weather and cattle prices.

It took an unusual person to do this kind of work. The cattle barons had to be smart and tough. Those were givens. But there was another essential quality: They had to embrace uncertainty and enjoy the challenge of moving men and animals across a broken, often hostile terrain.

Charles Goodnight was perhaps the prototype.

He was born on a farm in southern Illinois in 1836, but his family moved to the Brazos River country of Texas in 1845. It was still wild land, filled with buffalo and Indians and half-wild longhorns. To a nine-year-old boy, a new world had been opened.

Goodnight's official schooling was over. Instead, he learned the cattle business - the basics of branding and driving, but also the subtler skills that were no less important. From watching the flight of mud swallows, he knew the direction of watering holes. He knew how to slake his thirst by sucking on a bullet, and how to make prairie dog stew.

In 1856, he and a stepbrother began learning the business of ranching by tending to 430 cattle on the neighboring C V Ranch. It was an arrangement similar to sharecropping; in exchange for their work, they got to keep every fourth calf. After four years, they had nearly 200 head of cattle.

But before Goodnight could really get going, the Civil War arrived, with Texas part of the Confederacy. Goodnight avoided most of the bloodshed by joining the Texas Rangers to protect the state's western flank from Indian attacks. As the war drew to a close, Goodnight was discharged and began to reclaim his herd and that of his former employer, which had grown to some 5,000 head. By some accounts, there were 5 million longhorns in the state.

Now came the first gamble. Goodnight and his stepbrother bought the whole C V herd on credit. As the war ended, they had 8,000 head, and it was time to start making their investment pay off. Goodnight wanted to drive the cattle to Colorado, where booming silver and gold mines - and rising military presence - might mean a good profit. It was more than he and his brother could handle. They needed a partner. Oliver Loving, a well-known cattleman with a firm knowledge of the ranch and range was their man. He was already a veteran of cattle drives, having moved herds up the Shawnee Trail before the Civil War.

To avoid the Comanches, still a dangerous presence in Texas, Goodnight proposed a counter-intuitive route to the Denver area. They would first head southwest into New Mexico and then north into Colorado, with the Rockies on their western flank. It was brilliant but risky. Loving was in.

Loving and Goodnight left in June 1866, with 2,000 head of cattle and eighteen men, riding toward the headwaters of the Concho River, near the present town of Big Spring, Texas. They watered the herd to the point of bursting, then they were off on what they knew would be a desperately tough stretch.

Goodnight and Loving drove the herd non-stop, and the cows began dropping. On the third night, the lead cattle smelled the Pecos River and began bolting for it. The stampede would leave 100 cattle dead, adding to the 300 that had died en route. But those losses were quickly forgotten. The herd was sold in two groups: at Fort Sumner in northern New Mexico and then in Denver. Goodnight headed back to Texas with $12,000.

The partnership, though, didn't last. The following year, Loving was shot in the arm and side by Comanches in southern New Mexico. He died after a squeamish doctor refused to perform an amputation that might have saved Loving's life.

Despite Loving's death, Goodnight continued for several more years to drive cattle along what was called the Goodnight-Loving Trail. But by 1870, he decided to move his herd closer to market and eliminate the drives. He bought a sprawling piece of property near present-day Pueblo, Colorado, along the front range of the Rockies.

There, Goodnight thrived at first, but it peeved him how much he paid in interest to his creditors. In a plan to beat them at their own game, he decided to get into the banking business and joined an outfit called the Stock Growers Bank of Pueblo. The timing was unfortunate. The bank opened for business in the same month as the great crash of 1873. Goodnight said his losses "wiped me off the face of the earth." In an effort to rebound, he bought too much cattle, and the result was further ruin, enough to keep any other man on the canvas for good.

It was in this despair that Goodnight formed a new plan to find another piece of property, another stake. The Texas Panhandle had been largely ignored country - seen as uninviting, and bypassed by the swarms of settlers looking to make a new life in the West. But it was there that Goodnight saw Palo Duro - and then made it his own, with corrals and a small house beside a creek.

His dream to expand and build another cattle empire required money, and Goodnight found investors in John and Cornelia Adair. John was an Irishman, heir to a fortune. Cornelia was from a well-to-do New York family that included bankers and politicians. They arrived in Palo Duro in 1877 to learn about ranching life. Goodnight was happy to instruct - at a price.

Adair invested nearly $500,000 in the ranch and agreed to pay Goodnight an annual salary of $2,500 to run it. As part of the arrangement, the ranch's brand would be "J A." With those funds, Goodnight began buying and claiming more land, eventually controlling all the property in the canyon. He built a small village of some fifty houses, including a stone home for the Adairs when they came to visit. There was also a dairy, a blacksmith, even a tin shop. In just a few years, the J A Ranch had 100,000 head of cattle, and John Adair had cleared a profit of $512,000.

Goodnight's expansion at Palo Duro wasn't unusual. It reflected the looming battles across the Plains as the cattle business kept growing and ranches, once isolated islands, started rubbing up against each other.

Grazing land was important, but water was everything. A cow might drink up to thirty gallons a day. So a cattleman who held control of a watering hole or a stretch of river could conceivably claim the surrounding property up to ten miles away – as far as the average cow could walk back and forth in a day.

Over time, an informal rule book was created to determine whose claims were the most solid or least dubious. It went by different names: cow custom, range privilege, possessory rights, accustomed range, and range rights. They all dodged the essential theft of the land from the government, but lent an air of legitimacy to the whole structure. Possessory rights, for instance, meant that government land appropriated and sold by a rancher carried with it the right of occupancy. And if Federal officials didn't show up to challenge such rights – and they seldom did - local courts were happy to recognize them.

These arrangements were the key to wealth. For example, when the Coad brothers in western Nebraska sold ranch property for $913,853, they were selling only 527 acres that they actually owned. Most of what they sold consisted of possessory rights to more than 140,000 acres, some 220 square miles.

In the early years, the claims didn't extend to exclusive use of the land. In fact, most cowboys and even some ranchers believed that the Code of the West made the whole outdoors free to everyone. But the arrival of barbed wire - which made it possible to build strong, cheap fences - soon changed that ethic. The cattle barons fenced in their pastures and watering holes and began keeping everyone else out. Barbed wire became a menacing and permanent hedgerow. The Arkansas Valley Cattle Company helped fence more than 1 million acres of public land in Colorado. Small farmers found their land completely fenced in. Lesser ranchers were cut off from crucial watering holes.

The U.S. government encouraged settlers to cut down fences, and an unlikely alliance of rustlers, homesteaders, and small ranchers obliged. Two days after Texas cowman R. A. David fenced in a 1,000-acre pasture, he found the wire cut in 3,500 places. The *Galveston News* reported in 1883 that twenty miles of fence put up by the Hickey Pasture Company had been hacked to bits by neighbors who needed the water inside it. The barons responded with the warning that such actions would be met with violent resistance, and shooting escalated into range wars. It was all an outrage and an affront to the politicians in the East. President Grover Cleveland ordered federal officials to prosecute the illegal fencers, and slowly the barbed wire that restricted public access to public lands began to be dismantled.

Not surprisingly, the barons did not sit idly by. They used their hired hands and friends – as well as anybody else they could control - to file homestead claims to the public lands. Then the cattlemen had the filers convey the property into their own holdings. Often, the cattle barons strong-armed local legislatures into empowering them with the tools and authority of the police; this allowed them to choose which laws to enforce and which to ignore.

On the Spur Ranch, a half-million acres in Texas, an employee shot a rancher suspected of cattle rustling. Other offenders might fall into the hands of vigilante groups, who stalked the night to dole out frontier justice. In the morning, without so much as a hearing, the guilty would be found hanging from trees - all in the name of law and order.

Even Charlie Goodnight blessed this questionable justice. Supposedly, when his wife expressed dismay at a vigilante hanging that used a telegraph pole as the tree, Goodnight replied, "Well, I don't think it hurt the telegraph pole." What she didn't know was that Goodnight had approved of the hangings.

This wasn't an isolated incident. The cattle barons often organized and sponsored the vigilantes, and winked when they overstepped. Some vigilance committees were actually muscle for the big ranchers. One night in 1879, night riders hanged a prostitute and a saloon-keeper whose primary crime had been to set up small homesteads on land coveted by the powerful cattlemen.

By 1880, the Great Plains from the Canadian border south through Texas were home to 11 million head of cattle. The land had been divvied up like a deck of cards. It was brimming with opportunity, with plenty of honest men, but also plenty of men who weren't above a little truth-stretching to service their greed. Ranching was business, and a head for numbers was as important as being good with a branding iron. The cattlemen were no longer looking for mavericks; they were trying to round up investors. And the cattlemen were often less than truthful in enticing wealthy investors to enter the business.

A brochure produced by West Texas cattlemen showed steamboats on what they called the Pecos, a navigational impossibility since the river was nothing more than a swift and shallow stream just 100 feet wide. The governor of what was then Wyoming territory boasted improbably that the dry climate hindered the conduction of heat, allowing animals to stay warmer in winter and reserve energy for growing.

Many foreign investors seemed eager to accept the sales pitches. They were swayed by books such as *Cattle-Raising on the Plains of North America*, published in 1885 by a German immigrant named Walter Baron von Richthofen, who was an uncle of the Red Baron of World War I. Wealthy and friendly, Richthofen asserted that the cattle business was as easy as picking apples.

"There is not the slightest element of uncertainty," Richthofen wrote. With a dizzying display of questionable statistics, he showed how 100 cows could become, within a decade, nearly 3,000 strong and a profit machine. Among other facts, the baron ignored the weather, the incidence of stillborn calves, as well as the many expenses that were part of the cattleman's budget. Other "experts" gave similarly rosy forecasts.

A surprising number of successful Eastern businessmen invested in the cattle business. They included William Rockefeller of Standard Oil; Chicago meat packer Nelson Morris, who had a 250,000-acre ranch he never visited; and Gordon Bennett, editor of the influential *New York Herald*. "With little distortion, it could be said that the membership of the Union Club of New York, the Harvard Club of Boston, and the Union League Club of Chicago controlled the major portion of Eastern capital in the range cattle industry," wrote Professor Gene M. Gressley of the University of Wyoming.

The cattlemen also fanned out across the Atlantic, visiting Dundee, Edinburgh, and London to tout the riches to be found on America's Great Plains. It was difficult, of course, for European investors to see what they were investing in. They had to rely on the pitchmen. It was an arrangement, according to the *Scottish Banking and Insurance* magazine, that was "all in favor of the vendor and most disastrous to the buyer."

Among the great spreads built with a thumb on the scale, the Swan Land and Cattle Company stands out as a singular tale of deception. The Swan ranch was commonly called "The Two Bar," after its brand, which looked like the modern equal sign. It was based in eastern Wyoming, on a piece of land that was bigger than the state of Connecticut.

The cattle company began as the dream of cattle baron Alexander Hamilton Swan, who had been raised and educated in Pennsylvania. He arrived in Wyoming in 1873 and began assembling his herd and range along the Big Laramie River. Within a few years, he consolidated his holdings into three cattle corporations along the Chugwater and Sybile creeks that flowed into the Big Laramie.

Hoping to expand, Swan sought out investors in

Europe, where it was cheaper to borrow money. As he looked for partners, he painted a highly optimistic view of the Two Bar. It wasn't quite a lie, but it wasn't quite the truth. ("In our business, we are often compelled to do certain things, which, to the inexperienced, seem a little crooked," Swan once said.)

Scottish investors bought his business for $2.4 million and kept Swan on as a salaried manager. The Scots told other investors that the future was bright, writing in a prospectus that "the business of Cattle-raising in the Western States of America is now acknowledged to be highly remunerative."

The new owners then went on a spending spree, first buying three small ranches to give them control over the Chugwater and Sybile watersheds. In 1884, they doubled down, paying $2.3 million for 550,000 acres of Union Pacific land to the west. Big as a steer himself, Goodnight was not a man to be trifled with. Eventually, they held dominion over rangeland totaling 3.25 million acres.

Swan Land was an enormous enterprise, controlling so many herds that it needed to publish a book of all the different brands used on the spread. The company paid top wages, as much as $45 a month, and promised men plenty of horses and dessert with their dinner every day. Dividends for 1883, 1884, and 1885 averaged a fat 25 percent a year – far higher than a cattle ranch normally could expect. The ranch also put on rodeos to entertain its Scottish owners, and one cowboy, soon to be famous under the name Butch Cassidy, showed off his sharp aim with a pistol.

But the overseas investors soon discovered that the showboating had its costs. One of the owners of Swan Land had done his own calculations - and discovered that he and his colleagues had received fewer cattle than they had paid for. Winter storms killed off a sizable portion of the herd, and then Swan himself went bankrupt in a separate investing scheme.

Swan's Scottish directors fired him as manager and sent in one of their own, a man named Finlay Dun, to get to the bottom of the mess. Dun began by figuring out the true size of the herd and then squaring that number up against the sales and birth records. The best estimate is that the Scots paid for 32,000 head that they never received, a swindle approaching $500,000. Eventually, while Swan himself sank into further poverty, the dour Scots restored the Two Bar to financial health.

The hazards for big investors went beyond cattlemen who cooked the books. Ranching was different from running most other businesses. One operation endured an epidemic of sunburned udders from light reflected off snow, which caused the afflicted cows to resist suckling calves. In addition, there were cattle rustlers and Indians making their final stand.

Despite it all, foreigners kept showing up, in the process creating some of the biggest cattle spreads in the West – and living the high life along with it.

One Scot, Murdo Mackenzie, assembled his Matador Land and Cattle Company in Texas, Montana, and the Dakotas. Mackenzie lived like a true baron in mansions in Denver and Trinidad, sent a son to Princeton, and traveled widely.

Other foreign barons lived equally opulent lives. German-born Conrad Kohrs had gotten into the cattle business on the back end, selling beef to miners in Montana. Eventually, he acquired some 65,000 head of cattle and a rangeland of a million acres in eastern Montana. For culture, his wife took the train east to New York, where she enjoyed the Metropolitan Opera.

Other Europeans dressed their servants in fancy uniforms and made sure that cut flowers were sent to their estates. *The Economist* magazine noted the fondness of Englishmen for building "castles on the prairie."

Perhaps the most impressive ranch built with foreign capital was the X I T, financed with British money, in the Texas Panhandle just west of Palo Duro. It was said that the X I T Ranch had to buy barbed wire by the carload. The property was strung along 200 miles, including parts of ten counties, on the Texas-New Mexico border.

In the late 1880s, the X I T and another cattle outfit put together a second ranch operation in Montana nearly as large as the original. It sprawled over 200 miles in the broad fork of the Yellowstone and Missouri Rivers. To create a secure passage between their two giant holdings, the X I T's owners had acquired nearly 900 miles of trail wandering through seven states. As the first set of drovers left Texas with a herd bound for Montana, X I T General Manager A. G. Boyce gave the marching orders clearly: "Keep your eye on the North Star and drive straight ahead until you can wet your feet in the waters of the Yellowstone."

But sheer size was no guarantee of peace and prosperity or even political clout. In 1884, the vast open range of Wyoming was the domain of about twenty prosperous ranchers. Slowly, however, small homesteaders filled the area, competing for the sources of water and sometimes stealing the unbranded calves. Tensions increased when drought and severe blizzards killed thousands of cattle in 1886 and 1887. At the same time, cattle prices fell sharply and several of the barons went bankrupt.

The homesteaders greatly outnumbered the cattlemen, and when they were accused of rustling, it was all but impossible to get juries to convict. The big ranchers now became more aggressive in appropriating land and water rights, and hired range detectives to crack down on rustling. They formed a Stock Growers Association and banned small ranchers from the annual roundup. But the cattle barons' problems continued, and the small farmers and ranchers now had the political edge.

Finally, in 1892, the Stock Growers Association hired a force of fifty "Regulators" from Texas, including several known killers, to go after the alleged rustlers. That set off what was called the Johnson County Range War. The Regulators shot and killed the appointed leader of the small farmers, Nate Champion. In response, Sheriff Red Angus led a posse of 200 men – homesteaders, small ranchers, and disgruntled cowboys – to round up the Regulators. The posse surrounded them, along with some of the cattle barons, at a ranch on Crazy Woman Creek. The standoff might have turned deadly, but the Sixth Cavalry soon arrived to rescue the cattlemen, who were taken into protective custody.

The twenty-three Texas gunslingers captured at the ranch made bail and promptly left town. The local defendants were to be prosecuted, but material witnesses disappeared and impartial jurors couldn't be found. In time, the charges were dismissed. The alleged rustlers continued to be hanged for the next decade, and scattered violence persisted until the Johnson County War faded into history.

But despite the battles, hangings, bad investments, and empire-building, the cowboy and his place in the business of cattle lived on.

3
A COWBOY'S LIFE
"COLDEST PLACE I EVER SAW."

It was toward the end of the Cowboy Era that the famous journalist Richard Harding Davis toured the Great Plains. True to his trade, Davis was also a close observer of the land. He wrote of the disconnection between the range, where the cows roamed, and the ranch, where the cowboys lived. "The inhabited part of a ranch, the part of it on which the people who own it live, bears about the same proportion to the rest of the ranch as a lighthouse does to the ocean around it," he wrote.

Davis was correct. A ranch was mostly a sea of grass - rolling and windswept - where the cattle roamed, unaware of their fate. The small, settled section where the cowboys lived was lacking any pretense of grandeur. The buildings were often raw and unfinished. Even as the cattle business grew into permanent, year-round operations, the living quarters for cowboys were places where comfort was at best an afterthought.

Many of the cowboys lived in bunkhouses. These came in different designs. There was the so-called "saddle-bag" layout, where a living and sleeping area was connected to a cooking and eating area by a narrow dogtrot - a passageway that doubled as a convenient place to hang saddles, bridles, and other gear. More often, the bunkhouse was a separate building, little more than a shack made from flimsy weatherboard or cottonwood logs. Sometimes, in an effort to create more space, the cowboys put boards in the ceilings to create a small attic, which one cowboy said was the "coldest place I ever saw."

If there was one thing shared by all bunkhouses, from Montana to Texas, it was their smell. It was a combination of sweat, manure, leather, and tobacco, perhaps with a hint of burning lamp oil and skunk tallow. Along with the stench was, well, the mess. The floor was the closet, with clothes discarded near beds. (One historian joked that the arrangement eliminated the chance of the garments falling down or getting lost.)

Despite the squalor, some ranch hands could get downright sentimental about the camaraderie of the bunkhouse. There were nights spent telling stories or perhaps singing a few verses from *There's an Empty Cot in the Bunkhouse Tonight*. That song, about a cowboy who gave his life to bring a calf in out of the cold, often brought a tear to even these range-hardened men:

> There's an empty cot in the bunkhouse tonight
> There's a pinto's head hangin' low
> His spurs and chaps hang on the wall
> Limpy's gone where the good cowboys go.

The other constant in the bunkhouse was boredom, particularly during the winter when harsh weather and reduced daylight could keep the men indoors for long stretches.

To combat boredom, the men pooled their money to buy reading materials, usually magazines and catalogues. The pages were read and reread and passed from bunk to bunk. Eventually, the pages might become wallpaper, pasted to the interior of the bunkhouse in an ineffective effort to defeat the drafts. Cattleman Dennis Collins recalled once being stuck with nothing to read other than some material from a patent-medicine company.

When they got tired of reading, the cowboys played cards. That wasn't possible on all ranches, since some owners frowned on gambling. But allowed or illicit, these games often involved stakes like wolf scalps, which served as an informal currency across the plains.

Culture made only fleeting appearances.

Now and then a cowboy whose previous life had included a bit of education might quote some poetry. But the use of big words - and other attempts to impress a bunkmate - were met with derision or even a pistol shot to the dark corner of the bunkhouse.

Despite the close quarters, the bunkhouses were often places for gunplay. Some of it was just passing the time. Guns were not only weapons; they often doubled as toys. One evening at a ranch in southern Colorado, the hands were looking at magazine pictures pasted to the walls. "Soon, out came the pistols," wrote one historian. "The first shot got Benjamin Franklin square in the eye, reported a cowhand who took part. Another cowboy decided: 'That pretty girl's got a nose that's too long' and proceeded to snick off pieces of it with well-placed shots."

Cowboys accepted the bunkhouse as one more fact of life. Just as with everything else on the ranch, they knew, they came a distant second to the animals. The purpose of a ranch wasn't to make cowboys comfortable; it was to raise cattle and get them fat and profitable.

Beyond the bunkhouse lay thousands of acres of land and months spent in the saddle performing dozens of menial, dirty or dangerous chores.

The job of keeping the cattle healthy never ended. In the summer, blowflies descended upon the herd, laying eggs in open wounds, including those that resulted from brands or castrations. The eggs became screwworms, large maggots nearly an inch long that caused excruciating pain and sometimes death. The key to prevention was treating the wound before the flies got there.

To daub the wounds and kill the screwworms, the men carried bottles containing a powerful mixture of carbolic acid and axle grease, among other ingredients. These crude remedies occasionally turned out to be more lethal than the ailments. A cowboy, for example, once treated a skin disease by sprinkling kerosene on the hide of some cows - a widely accepted remedy. Everything was fine until one cow got loose and ran through a branding fire. It then ran to the others, and they caught fire as well. Twenty head were lost.

There were other unpleasant tasks the cowboys had to deal with.

To escape the swarms of flies, the cattle sought water, wandering in the spring and summer into the deepest mud they could find. Then they could get stuck, sometimes for days before they were found. The cowboys tried to pull them to solid ground, hoping the beeves still had enough strength to stand on their own.

De-horning the beasts was another arduous task. As in branding, the animals had to be restrained to endure the process, which also required patience and the proper tools. The cattle were corralled and led one by one through a chute, where the ranch hands used saws to take off the horns. For the oldest bulls with the hardest horns, a saw literally wouldn't cut it. Their horns were chopped off, like limbs on a cottonwood tree. De-horning was terribly painful for the bulls, as the nerves in the quick of the horn were severed. (Think of having a root canal without anesthetic.)

The risks and hazards of a cowpuncher's life seemed endless. In the summer, with the sun high in the sky and rain but a fond memory, the cowboys kept a watch for fires. Driven by the relentless wind, a prairie fire could sweep across entire counties, killing the cattle and searing the grazing land. The cowboys hitched themselves behind crude plows to construct firebreaks - a set of furrows in the tough prairie sod, stripped of fuel in the middle – to block or at least slow the flames. One cowboy estimated he plowed 150 miles of firebreaks in a single summer. It was an endless and nearly Sisyphean task. The range was too large and the threat of fire always too near for the cowboys to ever feel safe.

If the firebreaks didn't hold, the cowboys were forced to take other measures. Fighting a fire at a ranch in the Texas Panhandle, a group of cowboys first used wet gunny sacks and slickers and brooms to try to snuff it out. When that failed, they shot a steer, skinned him on one side, tied ropes to his legs, and dragged his bleeding carcass across the fire line like a wet rag. Supposedly, the horses dragging the animal had to step carefully to keep from burning their hooves.

While a fire could destroy an expanse of prairie in a single blaze, the more insidious problem was overgrazing.

As the cattle business boomed, ranchers often packed more cattle on the land than the grass could support. That would necessitate a drive - not to market but to richer pastures. It took time and manpower, and cattle on the move weren't cattle getting fat. For many cowboys, inspecting the grass became as important as scouring the horizon for fire or rustlers.

These small cattle drives were concentrated versions of the main event, with the same challenges: cows that didn't want to be driven - and some cowboys who weren't up to the task.

An exasperated trail boss named S. P. Conrad wrote this report on moving cattle across the Bitterroot Range separating Montana from Idaho: "I went as far as the Summit & Made up my mind that we could never drive the Cows with their calves & returned & sold them (the calves) at $4.50 per head.

He then got the remaining herd to Missoula, Mont., despite most of his crew quitting when the going got tough. But Conrad had a solution. "I intend to hire a full crew & kick out every son of a bitch that has the belly ache," he wrote.

It wasn't just overgrazed pastures that prompted cattle drives. Water was critical as well, especially when streams dried up in the summer.

In 1854, the wind-driven water pump was invented, and its eventual adoption across the Great Plains helped change the routine of a cowboy's work day. The pumps pulled water out of the great aquifers that lay below the plains, creating permanent sources of water in tanks at the foot of a windmill. As a result, water became less of a factor in forcing cattle drives, and ranches gained some greater level of permanence.

That development, in turn, led ranchers to control the herds - at least loosely – through the extensive use of barbed wire. For cowboys, that meant new jobs - and new tools to go with those chores. "A whole lot of sorry things can happen to a fence," one old-timer quipped.

A new category of cowboys sprang up to service the fences. They were called pliers men, and they rode their horses along the boundaries with a pouch full of staples, a roll of spare wire, and a tool that was both nippers and hammer. Each man might be in charge of ten to fifteen miles of fencing. He would be responsible for repairing missing or sagging wire and resetting the stones that were sometimes used to anchor the fence posts.

Invariably there were other jobs that arose. A pliers man might have to drive cattle to a better grazing area or pull some porcupine quills from a calf's nose.

Fixing windmills was another job – and it took at least two men to do it. The standard mill was thirty-two-feet high, and the gears and bearings inside the housing needed to be kept well-greased. Other repairs were more complicated. The sucker rods, which transferred the power of the blades to the plungers in the well casing, frequently broke. That could be diagnosed from a distance; the unrestrained blades whirled wildly and dangerously, as if demented. The fix involved pulling out the rod and plunger, then mending the break and reinstalling the whole contraption.

With jobs like that, injuries were common on the range. Medical care was not.

Health care was still in its infancy in most of the United States, and the isolation of the prairie just compounded the problem. Doctors were scarce, and medical treatment often relied on luck, folk wisdom, and improvisation. One ranch hand claimed he fixed a sprained ankle in a few days by wrapping it in brown paper and soaking it with vinegar. Another cowboy treated a deep cut by making a poultice out of his chewing tobacco - a favorite remedy for bee stings and just about everything else. At a ranch in New Mexico, a man with a fever and side pains was told to drink a potion containing Thribble H Horse Liniment and sleep with his head facing north. There's no record of the result.

Serious injuries might require fetching outside assistance. But even in those cases, the remedies were sketchy. A Texas cowboy who tore up his leg on barbed wire had a small-town doctor sew up the wound. There was no anesthesia available, so the doctor had his assistant, a stout young man who weighed 200 pounds, sit on the cowboy during the procedure.

The dangers of the cowboy business were bookended with activity that was far less strenuous than, say, stretching barbed wire or fixing windmill blades - and sometimes downright humble. Some of it even required extended periods of being dismounted from a horse. One cowboy spent three weeks doing nothing but gathering piles of dried cow manure, the fuel of the prairies, which added a tangy odor to everything from clothes to food. Since most such deposits had scorpions underneath, this task also meant wearing gloves and paying constant attention.

Other chores might include trapping turtles in a watering hole, raising chickens or working as a dairyman. A Colorado cowboy with the nickname Lasso Bill, who had his own small ranch, wrote about his daily responsibilities: "I picked six good milk cows out of the herd of range cattle and drove them into the corral and milked them twice a day. I had to rope these cows every time I milked them, snub their heads close to a post and then tie their hind legs together before they would submit to being milked. I made butter and sold the extra butter, milk, and buttermilk, also eggs, to passing immigrants. I had a flock of chickens at the ranch, and they furnished me several dozen eggs a day."

These farm chores were a direct result of the increasing modernization of the cattle business, which transformed it from one of nomadic wandering to a more anchored operation. Ranch hands might spend months harvesting hay or other crops. The same windmills that pulled water for the cattle could also divert the flow to irrigation. The ranches began growing corn and melons alongside hay, which was still the principal crop and was often stacked in staggering mounds the size of small hills.

For the cowboys, the work still slowed down in the winter. Come late November, two-thirds of them would have been let go and told perhaps to come back in a few months for the spring roundup and the summer cattle drives. Mostly bachelors, the unemployed men might move to town and cram into a rooming house with others in the same situation. The ambitious ones might take a temporary job tending bar or shoeing horses.

When cabin fever struck, the men might take off for a few days or weeks, riding the "grub line," a tradition across the frontier country. It involved riding from ranch to ranch in search of a free meal and an odd job or two. The grub-line riders weren't beggars; it was an honorable pursuit. For ranchers on isolated spreads, a grub-line rider was a welcome diversion - a fresh face hopefully carrying news from the outside world in exchange for a hot meal. And if nobody was home when a grub-line rider showed up, the code of the prairie condoned coming inside, making a quick meal, and bedding down for the night.

Cowboys who stayed on the ranch during the winter could be kept somewhat occupied cutting firewood to feed the insatiable stoves for cooking and heating. That was easy compared to other jobs, such as hauling stone from a quarry to build a house for the ranch manager or working a seam of coal with pickaxe and shovel.

One Texan, a man named Bob Haley, spent a winter rendering the fat from nearly a dozen cattle to make tallow to be used in the lamps. He later reported that the light given off was pretty good and that biscuits rolled in tallow were extra flavorful.

There were no cattle drives in the winter, of course, but that didn't mean that the cattle were forgotten. If nothing else, the beasts had to be kept alive until the weather improved – an outcome that was far from given.

The animals often acted in perverse ways. They stood in one place, stubborn and hungry, rather than look for food. Clad in buffalo coats, the cowboys rode the range to look for places where the wind had swept the snow from the grass and then tried to drive the cattle in that direction. Cows wouldn't eat snow, and when the watering holes froze up, the cowboys had to break through the ice to clear a drinking spot.

Blizzards were the worst hazard. In the swirl of white, the cattle were often be found with their eyes frozen shut and icicles hanging down from their muzzles like daggers. When they found a cow that was dying or already dead, the cowboys always tried to salvage something of value, usually the hide. But conditions meant they had to work with speed. "The only cows we could skin were the ones yet with circulation," explained cowhand Arch Sneed, assigned to the cattle-skinning detail on the X I T spread. "They were down and couldn't get up. We would cut their throats and skin them while yet warm. The ones which had been dead for some time were frozen so hard that we couldn't possibly skin them."

Cattle struggling in the cold attracted the attention of more than just ranchers. They were the frequent targets of wolves, which preyed on the animals during the winter when other prey grew scarce. Wolf hunting was an exciting - and potentially rewarding - diversion from the humdrum existence of the ranch. A cowboy might make $35 a month, plus expenses, to hunt wolves, in addition to getting a $5 bounty for each wolf scalp.

As the ranches grew larger, cowboys were assigned the duty of line riding, which involved patrolling the perimeter of the ranch. A rider might be responsible for a six- or eight-mile stretch of the boundary. Particularly in the days before barbed wire girdled the west, the line riders were responsible for making the owner's cattle stay inside the borders and the neighbor's herd stay out – not an easy task. A cowboy could spend the better part of a day trying to find a few lost steers and get them back to where they belonged, and as soon as he rode to the next section of the line, the herds often were mingling again.

Along with that general duty, line riders had a long list of other jobs, including keeping cows away from alkaline water, watching out for rustlers and predators, and branding any cattle that had somehow been missed at the roundup. In addition, they often had to chase the cattle off the railroad rights of way. If a train struck a cow, the line rider kept note of the resulting remains so the rancher could submit a bill for damages.

A line-riding assignment might last a few weeks, and the accommodations made the bunkhouse seem like a palace.

The camps might be a one-room shack of sod, or logs with a blanket for a door. In the worst cases, they were little more than a cave scratched out of the hillside. "We dug an open-topped rectangular hole into the South side of a slope near water," recalled a Texas cattleman. "Thus the back wall and a part of each of the two side walls were formed by the ground. The remainder were made of logs chinked with mud." The roof was made of dirt-covered logs, with a mound of earth along the rear edge to divert the water running down the hill and keep it from rushing in.

Typically, two men shared a line camp. It was a hard existence, removed from the fellowship of the ranch. One diary scrap, found in a Montana camp, summed it up:

> May 6th – arrived here. Lonesome as hell, but a good supper. Buffalo hump and onions.

Food was more than nourishment. It was another job, something to be mastered - and the cowboys made do with the tools and supplies they were given. They rolled out their pie dough with a whiskey bottle, and typically were responsible for hunting for their supper. If they brought anything from the main camp, it might be a can of tomatoes or an onion.

But riding the line also gave a man time to think. And for those who didn't mind the isolation, there was magic in the simple existence. Jim Christian, a Texas cowboy on Charlie Goodnight's J A Ranch in Palo Duro, wrote: "I loved to ride to a steep ledge, view the canyon at sunrise, to smell the dewy cedar, and listen to the mocking birds. . . . I learned to know the trees, shrubs, and flowers in their seasons and the signs and legends belonging to each. I have robbed the eagle's nest for sport and fed wild turkeys and quail the bread and beans from my table. I delighted in a plunge at the big spring, formerly a watering place of the Indians. The hoot of the owl and the howl of the coyote were music to my ears through the long night. My comrade was my horse. A fellow could spend lots of time petting, currying, and fooling with a horse."

Christian was an outlier. For most cowboys, a stint on line duty was the "life of a buck nun." They couldn't wait to get back to the relative hustle and bustle of the ranch.

There, the sources of entertainment could be brutal to man and beast. Bored cowboys sometimes buried a rooster up to its neck and then rode by, swinging down from the saddle, and jerking the bird from the ground. Other times, the cowboys might convene a kangaroo court and try a colleague on a trivial charge, such as being a braggart. The convicted were suitably punished, perhaps painfully spanked while bent over a wagon tongue.

Beyond the tomfoolery, life at the ranch offered other diversions, in particular the chance of seeing that rarest of ranch creatures: women. Most often, she was the wife of the owner or the foreman, which meant she was to be treated with the utmost respect. That was generally fine with cowboys. Across the range, the male-female ratio was often ten to one, and sometimes the women seemed to be spaced like train stations, fifty miles apart. Regardless of a woman's marital status, her mere sight was a treat.

Occasionally, cowboys were invited to dine at the main house with the boss and his wife. Perhaps there might even be a dance, for which creativity was required due to the shortage of women. Cowboys who offered to dance the female parts were known for the evening as heifer-branded. They wore an apron around their waists or a handkerchief on their sleeves to indicate their status for the festivities.

On the rarest of nights, the ranch hosted a real party - with wine, women, and entertainment. At a wedding along the Cheyenne River, a rancher named Fred Dupree threw a bash that went on for ten days. A hundred whites and 500 Indians consumed twenty gallons of whiskey, a keg of wine, thirty beeves, and four buffalo.

At the famed Matador Ranch near the Texas Panhandle, the cowboys showed up for a Valentine's Dance one year that was a fandango to end all fandangos. The cowpunchers were dressed in flannel and buckskin, some with watch chains braided from their beloved's locks. The bunkhouse had been scrubbed, aired out, and emptied to serve as the dance hall, and a fire was blazing. It is said that at midnight, the dancing stopped for a feast of ham, turkey, and chicken. Then the music started up again, and the stomping and whirling didn't end until the sun rose.

Then it was back to the saddle. The cattle were waiting.

4
THE ROUNDUP
"COVERING THE DOG"

The long winter had ended when the cattlemen arrived in Miles City in April 1886. Then, as now, it was a small town, nestled in the cottonwoods along the south bank of the Yellowstone River.

The ranchers were there for the annual meeting of the Montana Stock Growers Association. Despite the name, the event attracted cattlemen from as far away as Washington and Texas and even a few Canadians. Railroad men and stockyard owners also attended. There were two reasons for the gathering. First, it offered a few days of festivities to celebrate the cattle industry's collective good fortune. Second, it was an opportunity to plan the annual undertaking required to keep the herds straight.

It was roundup time across the Northern Plains.

The parties came first, and they were grand. A military band from nearby Fort Keogh, established in the wake of General George Custer's rout at Little Bighorn, led the opening-day parade. There were ladies in carriages, and cowboys whooping and hollering down the packed dirt main street.

Later came an elaborate lunch, and that evening, a ball took place at the Macqueen House, a lodge and tavern that was the community's social hub. There, military officers danced with the daughters of ranchers to music provided by a six-piece band. For the lowly cowhands, excluded from the affair, were other forms of entertainment. They drank at the saloons and played poker. At a discreet establishment called Turners Theater, young women in short skirts invited cowboys to go upstairs and "drink wine" or engage in pleasures of the flesh.

The men had much to celebrate. At the cattlemen's planning session, held earlier at Miles City's indoor roller rink and civic center, the group had managed to draft a working agreement for the 1886 Montana Roundup. This was no small feat. (Even today, the roundup is considered one of the most extensive in the cattle industry.) Vast in scale and scope, the roundup underscored the blend of ingenuity and hard work that was essential to the cattle business.

Roundups had once been informal, loose-knit undertakings. They were based on the idea that a cattleman needed to know his inventory.

In the Spanish territories of California and Mexico, the ranchers held rodeos, a predecessor of the roundup. Unlike what a rodeo now signifies, these events didn't involve roping and riding contests. In its original Spanish, the word rodeo meant an encircling and surrounding of the stock. The vaqueros, or Spanish cattle drivers, also searched for strays in the rough back country. In some cases, they planted a pole in the hard ground and coated it with salt and tallow, which drew cows from the thickets.

Early roundups in Texas were equally casual. A rancher might go on a cow-hunt every now and then to locate and brand his calves. But as the business grew, and the number of cattle multiplied, the jumble of brands required more coordination. Each rancher was expected to contribute manpower to help with the sorting.

Those events tended to be the exceptions. In the Southern Plains, the land was so harsh and lacking in vegetation that each ranch needed enormous acreage. As a result, the herds tended naturally to keep to themselves.

The Northern Plains were different. Here the land was lush, a well-watered carpet of grass. It belonged to everybody and nobody, and speculators began building enormous herds in Montana and elsewhere. As a result, overgrazing became a serious concern. Also, the cattle just wandered in this bovine paradise, intermixing herds and creating a logistical nightmare for the cattlemen. Ranchers had to go out in search of wandering cattle, and then drive them home, often over long distances. The exercise - and it was heavy exercise - was bad for business. As the cows walked home, they lost weight, decreasing their value. Worse, the skinny cows were often too weak to survive the tough winters on the plains.

Thus, cooperative herding and branding grew. Eventually, it would extend beyond the roundup itself, fostering a cooperative spirit that kept conflict to a minimum throughout the year.

The cattlemen in Miles City had every reason to plan hard and plan well.

A roundup on the Northern Plains wasn't as simple as putting a few salt licks here and there, and waiting for the cows to wander in. The roundup was being conducted over an area the size of Pennsylvania, some 40,000 square miles of snake-bite country and home to a million head of cattle. The land seemed flattish, but closer inspection revealed a terrain riddled with river beds, gulches, and small canyons - all places where cattle liked to hide.

The first order of business was assembling the herds. The calves were counted and branded. Many of the males were castrated, a process that made them relatively more docile and also helped them gain weight. Crude veterinary work, to a point, might be done on ailing animals. And finally, the cattle were returned to their rightful owners. (One estimate held that the Montana herds carried 4,000 different brands, jumbled like stones in the river.)

The men at the Stock Growers Association meeting divided the range into seventeen districts. True to the enormity of the task at hand, some of these pieces were still gigantic - the size of individual New England states. (The distances were considered manageable for a crew of a hundred men.) The districts rarely were neatly drawn. Instead, they were typically defined by water, bounded by the rivers that rushed out of the Northern Rockies and carved up the land. This was based on the theory that beeves were less likely to stray across major rivers, so most of the cattle in each district probably belonged there.

One of those parcels, known as District 8, was a sprawling triangle of a few thousand square miles bounded by the Yellowstone on the south and the Missouri on the north, down to the confluence of these rivers at the eastern end of the district. The Musselshell River, a tributary of the Missouri, made up most of the western boundary. The eastern section was flat, but it quickly gave way to more treacherous terrain. Among the ranchers working the district were those from the Circle Dot, the N Bar N, the L S, the J Lazy J, the Bow and Arrow, and the L U Bar, a new ranch established just the previous year.

The L U Bar's foreman was a cowboy named Waddy Peacock, and as the bosses in Miles City finished their convention, he headed back to the ranch to get things ready. He was joined by a young Texan, only eighteen, named Luke Sweetman. Together, they rode out some sixty miles to one of the L U Bar's desolate houses to rest up for the long weeks of work to come. In later years, Sweetman recalled those days with detailed clarity, and his written recollections of the 1886 roundup became a valuable window both for historians and admirers of the true cowboy ways.

As is often the case, the weather failed to cooperate. The spring rains were late, and the roundup's start had to be pushed back until late May, when the range greened up and lured the cattle out of the bottom lands.

Peacock and his team took advantage of the delay. They repaired saddles, lined up extra horses, and - perhaps most important - overhauled the chuck wagon. This work involved greasing the wagon's axles and hubs and finding a team of draft horses stout enough to pull it over the weeks ahead.

Finally, it was time to go. Peacock, Sweetman, and the other cowhands, along with the cook and his wagon, set out for a rendezvous near Miles City. The pace, to start, was slow and deliberate. The cowboys walked the horses to keep them fresh and conserve their energy; there would be plenty of gallops later. They made their way to Sunday Creek, which twists and turns in lazy half circles until it meets the Yellowstone ten miles above Miles City, just far enough away to discourage many thrill-seeking cowboys from making one last sortie into town.

The grassy benchland was alive with nearly 100 men and some 500 horses, pooled from across District 8. There were plenty of chuck wagons, each responsible for feeding its own crew – as well as hands from ranches too small to have their own operation. Along with the men who called District 8 home were cowboys from ranches outside the district. Known as "Reps" - short for representative - they were charged with retrieving the far-flung strays from other districts and returning them to the right ranch beyond District 8's boundaries.

The meet-up was like a reunion, since many of the men had worked together on other roundups. They greeted each other like long-lost friends. Proper names were optional; there was a cowboy called One-Eye Davis and another called Bean Belly.

In the center of it all and wearing a silver-bangled sombrero was Tom Gibson, who the barons had chosen as captain of the District 8 roundup. The foreman of the J Lazy J Ranch, Gibson was a stern but friendly cowhand, and now he sized up his men. While the cooks drove their wagons across the river and down to Miles City for provisions, Gibson let his men relax for a few days and enjoy themselves.

The prime daytime diversion was horse racing. It was a rowdy affair on hastily built tracks, with the mounts often trailed by onlookers yelling and shooting pistols. At night, the men wandered from wagon to wagon, sampling the food of the various cooks. Despite the curfew and the distance, some of them snuck off to Miles City for one last taste of civilization, including perhaps some time with Connie the Cowboy Queen, who often wore a dress that was said to bear every cattle brand from the Yellowstone to the Platte.

After two days of this, it was time for the men to get to work. Most of the cowboys hit their bedrolls early, stretching out on the ground before it got dark. A few hours later, the L U Bar's cook was shattering their sleep with words that flowed first like honey and then turned sharp and acrid as horseradish. "Come, boys, get up and hear the little birds singing their sweet praises to the Lord God Almighty," he sang. And when that didn't have the desired effect, he added, "Damn your souls, get up!"

There was breakfast, the smoke of the fire hanging in the chill air. And then the men assembled around Captain Gibson for their assignments. The roundup was about to begin.

District 8 was too big an area to tackle as a single entity, so Gibson's strategy was to split his men into two teams - one to comb the east, the other the west. The tasks were identical: to gather and brand the cows, including the calves, and split up the herds into groups to make it easier to return the strays. Cattle owned by ranches that lay ahead of the drive were to be assembled into a herd and delivered along the way, similarly to a mail route. Cattle found after the roundup had moved past their ranch became the responsibility of the reps, who assembled these strays into packs that a single cowboy could drive back to their home pastures.

Very quickly, a small herd of cattle was gathered, and the time came to brand the first unmarked calf of the roundup. The honors went to Buck Merritt, the foreman of the Bow and Arrow Ranch, where the roundup had begun. He roped a calf and dragged it to the fire. But before the brand could be applied, the cowboys needed to know which iron to put in the fire. Cowboy wisdom solved the problem: When a calf is roped and restrained, it cries for its mother, and the cow that responds signals maternity. It was a truism of ranch life. So when a cow with the Bow and Arrow brand wandered over to check on her bawling offspring, the cowboys called out the brand and burned the insignia into the calf's hide.

Next up was a calf whose distressed mother carried the brand of the Mankato Cattle Company. It was a ranch to the south; the animals had evidently swum across the Yellowstone. "Tarantula!" yelled Merritt, signaling for the script M brand of Mankato, which to some resembled a spider.

The branding ritual went on all day until the shadows grew long and the air was heavy with the sharp smell of the burned hair and skin of several hundred calves. When the obvious calves were dispensed with, the roundup crews divided and the real work began.

Sweetman headed west with a small group, including a chuck wagon, to scour rougher country for a smaller number of cattle. That crew was led by Al Popham, the foreman of the L S Ranch.

The larger group headed east, toward the confluence of the Yellowstone and the Missouri in the Dakota Territory. It contained upwards of sixty men and 400 or more horses. They could gather herds of 2,000 to 3,000 cattle at a time, working as a team to encircle an area of several hundred square miles. The men at the edge drove the cattle toward the center of the area, where others handled the sorting and the branding. The size of the operation and its economics of scale allowed some luxuries not available to smaller crews. These cowboys had tents, a choice of dinners each night, and even a hand whose sole job was to cut firewood, saving the men in the saddle from a thankless chore.

The men in Sweetman's smaller group awoke at 3:30. Then the horses were driven into an improvised rope corral and the men picked out their rides for the morning. In the dark, Popham mapped out the day's work, using a stick to diagram the plan, including where the day would end. That decided, the chuck wagon and the unclaimed horses set off for the noonday rendezvous.

The search for cattle was easy where the land was flat. There, the men would form a semicircle and drive the cattle toward the rendezvous, with the goal of eventually ending up somewhere close to the chuck wagon.

That was the theory, anyway. But Eastern Montana didn't always follow the rules. It was broken land, with less precision and predictability than initially presumed. The little streams ran like veins, and the cowboys rode the ridge and scoured the branches. On a typical morning, a cowboy might cover thirty-five miles, and then do it again in the afternoon, changing horses to keep up his pace.

It was hard land for rider and horse. They had to skid down hills on their haunches and make their way across rocky ledges. Always, the goal was to find the cows and to move them along with the herd. A cow in a ravine might see the man on horseback, toss its tail in the air, and then trot off to find company. In this way, small herds became big herds, and the roundup went faster. Speed was important, but thoroughness was everything. The ranchers had special disdain for a cowboy who made only a half-hearted attempt at flushing cattle from the hidden draws and sloughs across the range. Sweetman's crew was free of such lazy men; at the end of each day, the collected herd usually topped 1,000 head.

Generally speaking, the bulk of the cattle collected in a given area belonged to the rancher whose spread was closest. The line riders who circled endlessly on the borders of each ranch throughout the year saw to that. But as with a fisherman's trawling net dragging the bottom, the day's catch invariably contained a few surprises, and the cowboys crowded around the beeves to point out the oddities among the brands. The strays were always the most entertaining - some might have come from as far as Wyoming, and all that awaited them was a trip back home.

After dinner came the hard work of separating the collected herd. The cowboys corralled their range horses and selected mounts trained for cutting. These animals were nearly like border collies:

alert and intelligent and supremely focused on their task. It was said that a good cutting pony didn't need reins; knee pressure from its rider was sufficient. The cowboy could indicate which cow needed to be pulled from the herd, and the horse was on the steer or calf in an instant. The goal was to work quickly and unobtrusively so as not to spook the other animals.

A few years before the Great Montana Roundup, a Montana cowboy named Reginald Aldridge wrote this testament to the athletic poetry of a great cutting horse: "A horse that knows what is wanted goes quietly through the herd while you are looking for your brand. When you have singled out your animal and urged her gently to the edge of the herd, he perceives at once which is the one to be ejected. When you have got her close to the edge, you make a little rush behind her and she runs out; but as likely as not, as soon as she finds herself outside the herd, she tries to get back again and makes a sudden wheel to the left to get past you. Instantly your horse turns to the left and runs along between her and the herd so that she cannot get in. Then she tries to dodge in behind you. The moment she turns, your horse stops and wheels around, always keeping between the cow and the herd till she gives it up and runs out to the cut, where you want her."

The cows had good reason to dodge and weave.

Beyond the cut lay the branding fire, fueled with wood dragged from the banks of a nearby creek. It burned at a temperature known as campfire hot, turning the irons a dull red. Anything more would burn too deep. The goal was an even brand, one that burned through the hair, took off the outer layer of skin, and left behind an imprint that healed to the bright brown color of a new saddle.

The pace of the branding was often quick. A good crew could do 300 calves in an afternoon, although it is said that a crew along the Marias River in northern Montana branded 130 calves in a half hour.

Accuracy was as important as quickness. With the irons heating and the calves bawling for their mothers, it was easy to make a mistake that burned with permanency. When a calf got the wrong brand, it was corrected with a jaw brand that showed true ownership and cleared up any confusion when a rider or buyer saw a calf suckling from an animal that at first glance didn't appear to be its mother. Occasionally, a cow turned up with a brand that no one recognized, but that was uncommon.

Popham and the other foremen carried brand books, filled with pages of markings. The crews also carried the branding irons of the largest local ranches as well as an assortment of curves and straights for recreating the brands of far-flung operations. As a result, when the branding was all done, a rancher hundreds of miles away from Montana could wind up receiving cattle he didn't know he had lost.

There were other ways of marking cattle. Ears could be notched and cropped in a dizzying number of ways, known by such terms as "over hack," "sharp," and "steeple fork." And beyond that, occasionally, the dewlap - the skin under the throat - was cut so it hung down like a flag.

While the cowboys branded and separated, they were also inspecting the animals, and they treated those with sores or wounds as best they could with salves and ointments. Ill-tempered steers with long horns might be dehorned using clippers, axes, and saws.

There was a grim accounting method for all of this work: By day's end, buckets near the fire contained parts of ears, castrated scrotums, and the like. These served as a further check for the tallyman, who kept meticulous notes on the number of cattle serviced during the afternoon.

By this time, the herd was really several herds. There was the main grouping, which would move on the next day, with each animal eventually dropped off at its home ranch. There was the local herd, calves and mothers already at home, for which the trick was to keep them from rejoining the larger bunch. And then there was the throwback herd - the steers, cows, and calves that needed to be driven back to ranges that had already been passed.

The beeves in the smaller groups kept trying to join the big herd, and the cutting riders spent hours policing the animals to maintain order until the work was finished. Then, whooping and shooting in the air, they drove the local herd away, so it could graze in peace on its own land.

As the sun began setting, the crews prepared the camp for the night. The main herd was moved closer to the wagons, and then the men ate their final meal of the day. Some - after fifteen or more hours in the saddle - had night guard duty to keep the herd in one group. The rest bedded down until their turn to ride guard.

The bedroll was part sleeping bag – quilts wrapped in a tarpaulin - and part storage container. But it was also the one item a cowboy could call his own. A bedroll could hold, as Wild West author Will James reported, "tobacco sacks, cigarette paper, buckskin leather, a marlinespike, perhaps a picture of the cowboy's girl, some old letters, magazines, shirts, underwear, socks, a clean suit, an extra pair of boots, soiled clothes, a spare cinch, and a rope." The whole contraption might weigh 150 pounds, and its mighty stench was almost soothing to the man who had created it. Laid out under a clear night sky, a bedroll was a fine place to fall asleep listening to the soothing sounds of the prairie. One cowhand said it was so quiet, "You can even hear the ponies bite off the short, crisp grass and chew it."

While the cowboys seemed to get along, the cattle drives weren't without conflict. Because much of the land across eastern Montana belonged to the federal government, property rights were as iffy as on other Western ranges, created through custom and often enforced by six-gun.

As a result, while the Montana Roundup moved through the state, its cowboys were often followed by a crew originally out of Texas, known as the S T V outfit. The Montana association had denied the group's request to participate in the roundup because the S T V group had plunked 3,500 head of Texas cattle on land just north of the Yellowstone – trying to prevent others from using the land. Three years earlier, the ranchers who divvied up nearly 4 million acres in central Montana had published a notice: "We consider the said range already overstocked; therefore, we positively decline allowing any outside parties or any parties locating herds upon this range to join us in any roundup."

The federal agent for the area wrote his bosses in Washington that this was "quite as effective as fencing the entire tract." But it hadn't prevented the S T V group from trying to horn in.

Similar battles were waged up and down the

range. Consider the response to a Texas proposal to establish a national cattle trail between the Southern and Northern ranges. A Montana newspaper summed it up: "We-uns just got pie enough to go around and ain't got none to spare you-uns. See?"

The hardball tactics didn't always work. The S T V owner, John Conrad, just ignored the boycott and told his hands to follow Sweetman's crew at a close but safe distance. When the local herd was cut loose each afternoon, the S T V men looked over the stock and found a few of their own. They followed the cowboys when they rode their big circular routes in the morning, discreetly making themselves known, and picking up the S T V cattle as the roundup crew left them behind just as discreetly. The disdain for free-riding went only so far. A brand was a brand, and ownership was honored.

As Sweetman acknowledged, there was no way to keep a man from riding a rod or two away from the circle, "especially when he is armed." And as he noted, it was also a game within a game. "It all happened on Uncle Sam's land," he wrote.

When the roundup was drawing to a close, the crews that had worked the different districts joined together and made the final push to the finish line.

Sweetman had enjoyed his time as a rep. The job

was a cut above the typical roundup assignment, and it offered opportunities to mingle with lots of different crews. He and the others began working an area near the Missouri, along two tributaries named Squaw Creek and Hell Creek. It was rugged country, too rough for a wagon. The cattle were down there in the thickets, and through hard work in the saddle, were brought back to the herd. Many, Sweetman later recalled in his journal, had not been seen by a man for two years.

And that was it. The Roundup was over. The teams had found, roped, and branded more than a million head of cattle.

In truth, the process never seemed to end. It was assumed there was always another roundup on the horizon, but Sweetman and his fellow cowboys congratulated themselves on a job well done. In the parlance of the time and place, they had "covered the dog," finding every last secretive and stubborn head of cattle in the hardscrabble territory.

Writing in his journal in his later years, Luke Sweetman - no longer a callow eighteen-year-old - noted that it had been a "perfect job." He had done it well, and he had loved it.

5
THE LONG DRIVE
"A TEMPEST OF HORNS AND TAILS"

There are numerous accounts of the cowboy's life. But perhaps the best depiction of the day-to-day routine on a long trail drive can be found in a memoir written by Baylis John Fletcher, who documented his work on the legendary Chisholm Trail in 1879 when he was nineteen years old.

Fletcher was born to Texas pioneer stock in 1859. His mother died giving birth to him, and since his father had six other children to support, the new baby was taken in by his mother's parents, Ephraim and Harriet Roddy. The boy became the special charge of his maiden aunt, Ellen Roddy. After his grandparents died, it was Aunt Ellen who raised him.

Outgoing and handsome, Fletcher was good at riding, roping, and other cowboy chores. Eventually, he developed "trail fever," gripped by "the same spirit of adventure" that had led his grandparents to Texas from their home in South Carolina. But his protective aunt needed to be convinced to loosen her reins. After fierce objections and long arguments, Aunt Ellen finally agreed to let him make the long trail drive.

Tom Snyder, a member of one of the most prominent Texas cattle families, lived next door to Ellen Roddy in the frontier village of Liberty Village. And, to no one's surprise, Snyder hired young Baylis Fletcher onto a crew to drive a herd of cattle north in the spring of 1879.

This is Fletcher's journey and how he remembered it.

It's the first light of a June morning in the year 1879 on the old Chisholm Trail. Ten men are two months into the formidable job of driving 2,500 cattle through the wilderness to market north in Montana.

A fire lights up the battered chuck wagon and the figure of the cook, busy over his pots and pans. Surrounded by the silent forms of cowboys in their bedrolls, Baylis Fletcher sits up in his undershirt and groans. It has been only three hours since he finished his shift as one of the two men guarding the herd at night.

This morning, Fletcher's ankles are aching with a

kind of inflammatory rheumatism that he thinks he got recently from drinking "gyp water," the alkaline remnants of a dried-up prairie stream. His lower legs have swollen so badly that he had to slit the legs of his boots to pull them on.

The cattle are just beginning to stir, goading the crew into action. Fletcher and the other cowboys get dressed, stuffing the tails of their wool shirts into their belts. They wet their faces with water drawn from the barrel on the chuck wagon, and dry off with a community towel. Fletcher, who was raised by his aunt to be neat, runs a comb through his hair.

Besides the cowboys, there are three other crew members: George Arnett, the trail boss, always addressed as "Mr. Arnett;" Manuel Garcia, the Mexican cook; and Carteman Garcia, the wrangler, whose job was tending to the spare horses, doing chores for the cook, and gathering firewood. The cowboys are a changeable crew. A few of them will drop out a third of the way along the trail; others will stick almost to the end but miss the payoff. Those closest to Baylis Fletcher were Albert Cochran, Sam Allen, Anderson Pickett, Poinsett Barton, Stephen "Shug" Pointer, and the Russell brothers, Dick and Will.

So far, the herd has come 500 miles from where it started in southern Texas, just north of Corpus Christi, with 700 miles to go to reach southeastern Montana. The men are in the Indian Territory that separates the states of Texas and Kansas. Trail boss Arnett, a onetime Confederate soldier and Indian fighter, decides that he will push the herd about ten miles north to the South Canadian River, which runs from west to east through what will one day be Oklahoma.

The men are gulping the last of their hot, black coffee when the sun rises at a quarter past five, seeming to pop from a hole in the flat horizon. The wrangler, who has been out gathering the horses, now brings them in to an improvised corral: lariats tied to the wagon wheels and held at waist height by the cowboys. Meanwhile, the cowboys take turns picking one from their string of horses to use for the morning's work. Depending on the man and the character of the horse, this can be done either by throwing a lariat over the horse's neck or walking up and slipping on a bridle. Two men ride out to relieve the last guards, who gallop in to gulp down their breakfast and choose fresh horses for themselves.

The men throw their bedrolls into the chuck wagon. Manuel Garcia stows his chuck box and his smoke-blackened Dutch ovens in the wagon, too. The ovens clang together like discordant bells as the cook drives off behind Arnett to locate the noonday rendezvous. The wrangler follows with the remuda, the string of resting horses.

The early morning is leisurely, but at 9:00, it's time

to get moving. The men start to pinch the front of the herd of Texas Longhorns together - and get the animals ambling in a ragged line of march at perhaps two miles an hour. They encourage the movement with a low, gentle chant: "Ho, cattle, ho ho ho." The riders on the sides and the rear of the herd also nudge gently, pushing strays back into the mass and funneling it into a narrowing column.

This herd is made up mostly of cows and their calves being sent to Montana for breeding purposes on the new ranches swiftly expanding on the northern Plains. Such a herd doesn't drive easily, since the cows and their calves tend to wander and then call out for each other in mournful, organ-tone moans. Arnett has brought along a few steers, better natural marchers, to act as leaders. As the steers move to the front, the cows and calves follow, gradually picking up the pace. The column extends, narrows to a dozen head, and finally stretches out to a two-mile-long string of cattle, plodding four abreast.

This morning, Fletcher is stationed on the left flank of the herd, where the work is relatively pleasant. The point is a bit more difficult, keeping the animals on pace and direction; the worst job is bringing up the rear, called the drag. At the rear, the cowboys breathe the herd's dust through the bandannas over their faces as they chase down strays and chivvy the weak or lame cattle and orphaned yearlings to make them keep up with the herd. In the name of fairness, the men have arranged to rotate these posts.

This was an unremarkable day on the grandest and most challenging adventure in the repertoire of the cowboy life – the long trail drive.

The long drives were full of perils – stampedes, blizzards, hailstorms, prairie fires, lightning, raiding wolves, flash floods at river crossings. But this day brought nothing worse than the routine miseries of heat, thirst, exhaustion, aches and pains, and grimly monotonous food. The crew had started with the salt air of the Gulf of Mexico in their nostrils; by the time they smelled the pines of the Rocky Mountains, they would have spent four months in the saddle.

Such a grueling experience turned boys like Baylis Fletcher into cowboys through and through.

Why did Fletcher and others do it? A job, any job, was a prize in those hard years after the Civil War, but these wages were paltry by any standard. The cowboys got $30 a month "and found," meaning the food, such as it was. Arnett's pay as trail boss was $100 a month; the cook got somewhere between the cowboys and Arnett, and the wrangler a bit less than the hands. At the end of the drive, having taken advances here and there along the way, Fletcher would draw final pay of about $100, perhaps enough to buy a new hat and a fancy pair of boots.

But these were young men, mostly, and they were testing themselves against the unknown. They aspired to the cowboy fraternity and mystique, already a potent brew. They took a perverse pride in enduring hardships; when the chuck wagon ran out of salt, they could lick horse sweat from their saddles. They relished the comradeship of the trail, telling yarns around the campfire. And they appreciated the ever-changing beauties of nature and the occasional pleasure of finding sweet blackberries or catching fresh fish. Perhaps they even felt pride in herding the rivers of brown cattle streaming across the Great Plains – in being part of the epic taming of the American West.

(For the cattle barons, the trail drive was a way to get the animals to market at the least cost – all told, a penny a mile per head. If a steer cost $10 to raise and $12 on the long drive, a $40 market price brought a fat profit.)

Their testing ground was the Chisholm Trail. It was named for Jesse Chisholm, a Scots-Cherokee merchant who had set up a trading post on the Canadian River and carved a fairly straight, level wagon road, with shallow river fords, between his post and the settlements in south-central Kansas. In the first five years after the trail was first used to drive cattle in 1867, more than a million beeves passed over it.

The cowboys knew risks – the horse accidents,

lightning strikes, disease - were part of the bargain. They knew, too, that their lives took a lower priority than the safety of the cattle. Among trail bosses, the watchword was, "Look out for the cows' feet and the horses' backs, and let the cowhands and the cook take care of themselves." It was part of the bargain.

But the cattle baron of this drive was Fletcher's neighbor, Captain Tom Snyder, a drover who usually bossed his own drives. (This time, he had hired Arnett.) Snyder had a reputation as a pious man, who wouldn't let his hands curse and tried to keep them out of cow-town saloons and brothels. He was also a cautious man, who wanted his cattle well handled. Some drovers thought it was enough to hire one hand for every 400 cattle, but Snyder's ratio was one to 250. Unlike many other cattle bosses, he also supplied a remuda - a herd of saddle-broken horses - for the cowboys to use, as well as a stout wagon with a team of oxen to carry the cook, his gear, and the bedrolls.

Snyder had bought the horses for the remuda while the herd was still being assembled, and he chose them carefully. Cow ponies were nimble and intelligent but relatively small; half a day's work on the trail usually tired them out. As a result, each hand needed two horses for the day's work and another for riding guard at night. The ponies got at least a day's rest in the remuda between working stints, so each cowboy got his own string of eight horses at the start of the drive. Later, Snyder bought more ponies, bringing the total used on the drive to eighty.

The horses proved to have specialized talents. Some, like Fletcher's favorite Happy Jack, had good night vision and were best at night guard duty. Others were cutting ponies that knew how to separate individual steers from the herd without creating a fuss. At first sight, the men had to guess what they were getting. They drew lots to determine the order of choosing and then picked the horses one by one in rounds, like present-day athletes in a professional draft.

The drive had started in the first week of April; and at the same time, young Fletcher began taking the notes that would lead to his memoir. From the beginning, it was clear the cowboys were on a perilous journey that would take all the guts and stamina they could muster - and patience.

Arnett and his crew picked up the herd of 2,500 cattle at Green Ranch, just north of Corpus Christi, where Snyder had assembled them. When the herd was finally all present and accounted for, the hands ran them through a chute and the brand – "T L," for some reason – was applied by irons heated to a dull red.

The night before they hit the trail, the cowhands

hired some musicians and threw themselves a farewell party at the ranch. It was a stag dance, Fletcher wrote, with each man sashaying "in the warm embrace of another wearing spurs, leather leggings, and broad-brimmed sombreros."

All seemed to be in good spirits, but the drive got off to a nearly disastrous start. On the second day, while the cattle were being guided cautiously through the streets of the town of Victoria, an old woman flapped her sunbonnet at them to keep them out of her garden. The leading steers stampeded back through the following cattle, which took off in every possible direction. The townspeople sought refuge indoors as horns clashed in every street. It took the men two hours to stop the stampede, quiet the herd, and get the beeves lined up and plodding northward again.

As often happened with trail cattle, the longhorns were spooked by this first stampede; from midnight until almost dawn, they stampeded again and again at every ghost of an excuse. The hands spent all night in the saddle and were exhausted the next day.

The damage was compounded a few nights later. Fletcher and his fellow night watchman, Sam Allen, were warming themselves around a fire, against orders, when the herd suddenly took off again, directly toward them. They could only cringe behind an oak tree as the beeves swept past, so close that their horns slashed the bark off both sides of the tree.

A herd of longhorns in full stampede was a terrifying sight - "a tempest of horns and tails," as one cowboy put it. The cattle uttered no sound, but the thunder of hooves and the clashing of horns filled the air. In the turmoil, the animals could bruise, kick, and gore each other, and a cowboy who fell from his horse into that churning of hooves was almost surely doomed. The energy the cattle spent was amazing. A steer could lose fifty pounds in a four-mile run, and the heat given off by a stampeding herd, said one rancher, "almost blistered the faces" of the men riding on the downwind side.

When the horns stopped raking the tree, Fletcher jumped on his horse and raced to the head of the stampede. He managed to turn the cattle until they merged with the rear of the herd and milled in a circle, gradually slowing to a halt. This job was usually reserved for the most experienced cowhands, since turning a stampeding herd was a dangerous and difficult chore. Sometimes it would take several men, flapping slickers at the beasts and firing six-guns into the ground beside their heads, to persuade them to deviate from their line of charge and begin to circle.

The next morning, 100 cattle were missing. Four tough-looking men showed up and offered to hunt them down for a dollar a head. Arnett, figuring accurately that these men had started the stampede and probably already had the cattle, offered fifty cents. The men accepted, but came back with only sixty cows. Arnett's searchers found another twenty, but twenty were gone for good.

The herd stampeded again a few days later. This time, the cattle had bedded down for the night in a corral, one of the pastures that ranchers rented out to trail herds passing through settled country. There was no apparent cause for the stampede at all; the cattle just took off, breaking through the rails of the corral and giving everyone another sleepless night in the saddle.

In the commotion, Fletcher lost his hat, a cowboy's proudest badge of office. The next day, he found a general store that carried hats, but it was Sunday, and the owner refused to break the Sabbath. So Fletcher had to ride bareheaded all day and find another store on Monday. It proved fortunate that he did.

Two weeks later, as the cattle drive passed through central Texas, the sky opened up with a fusillade of hailstones as big as quails' eggs, which hit hard enough to kill birds and rabbits. Cowboys on the open prairie dreaded hail, which could get even larger than the stones in this storm. A hat offered some protection. But a man's only real defense was to dismount, strip the saddle from his horse, and crouch beneath it, leaving the horse to fend for itself. These hailstones raised such welts on the men's exposed arms that, a few days later, the skin sloughed off. While the storm lasted, the battered cattle drifted off the trail and scattered. When it was over, the men had to round up the herd and set it back in motion.

Luckily for Arnett and his crew, this hailstorm was the only one of the long drive. The T L herd was also spared blizzards, which could sweep down on Texas as late as May. In one spring blizzard in 1874, a trail crew was hit so hard that all seventy-eight horses in the remuda froze to death. The Longhorns, conditioned by centuries on the open prairie, were hardier.

Now the crew was approaching Fort Worth. With 6,500 citizens, it was the largest town on the Chisholm Trail in 1879 – a metropolis compared to the other stops. A group of salesmen from the downtown outfitting stores rode out to meet the herd and sell supplies, and the cowboys took the opportunity to play an elaborate practical joke. One of the older cowboys pretended to be the trail boss, and the drummers surrounded him, pressing him with cigars and whiskey to buy their wares. Then another cowboy galloped up and yelled at the impostor, as rehearsed, "The boss says come on you lazy cuss and get to work, or he'll turn you off at Fort Worth." The cowboys all howled at this rare feat of hoodwinking city slickers. Arnett, who had been watching with a smile, soothed any hurt feelings by buying two months' worth of provisions from the drummers.

The next hundred miles turned out to be two weeks of quiet weather and good grass, just right for getting the herd attuned to life on the trail and out of the stampeding habit. Life, for the cattle and crew alike, fell into a comfortable routine.

In the early mornings, the herd grazed for a few hours as it drifted northward alongside the trail. Starting at about 9:00 a.m., the cattle were nudged onto the trail for a steady trudge of four or five miles. Arnett rode ahead, scouting for good noonday pasturage where no other herds had recently grazed or bedded down. When he found it, he came back to the trail and rode in a small circle, as a signal to the point men leading the herd. Once he got their attention, he stood still in profile, with his horse's head pointing right or left to indicate which way the herd should turn. At about the same time, a curl of smoke appeared over the chosen spot, announcing that Garcia and the wagon had arrived and the noon meal – dinner, the men called it – was being cooked.

After a day's march of ten to twelve miles, at about 5:00 in the afternoon, the herd reached the place Arnett had chosen for the night. Far ahead of the lead steers, he marked the spot by waving his hat in slow circles around his head. When they reached that point, the cowboys eased the cattle off the trail to grazing and bedding grounds near the wagon, where Manuel Garcia was boiling his eternal beans and frying his bacon for the evening meal.

Though they were surrounded by cattle, the cowboys rarely got beef to eat. "Killing a beef on the trail was a great waste, as only a small part of the meat could be eaten before it spoiled," Fletcher explained in his journal. Just once, the T L crew killed a stray yearling steer that had joined the herd, and Manuel Garcia broiled as much meat as they could eat before it went bad.

The cook also boiled up a slightly longer-lasting batch of the gourmet dish known as "sonofabitch stew," with exotic ingredients that contrasted completely with more-typical fare like Pecos strawberries and overland trout. There were as many recipes for this dish as there were trail cooks, but it was likely to contain the animal's heart, tongue, and liver. Its flavor was enhanced by marrow gut, the partially digested contents of the tube connecting a cow's two stomachs.

Earlier and later on the drive, as it passed through settled land, Arnett might be able to vary the menu by bargaining with farmers along the route. If the herd spent the night in a farmer's pasture, it would leave an ample supply of cow chips for the next winter's fuel; in exchange, the farmer might provide eggs or fresh vegetables for the crew. If the farmer was lucky, a cow in the herd might choose his pasture to drop her newborn calf. (Longhorns gave birth at intervals of eleven months, which meant calves could arrive at any time of year). Since it couldn't keep up with the herd, the calf would have to be killed if not left with the farmer. And his gratitude for this addition to his livestock would be expressed in as many extra eggs and vegetables as he could spare.

But there were few settlers as the T L herd neared the northern border of Texas, and the daily routine became comfortable and familiar. The grass along the trail hadn't yet been overgrazed, and the summer heat had not become oppressive. So, for cows and men alike, the trek north became a kind of idyll.

But after this happy interlude, they came to the Red River, the northern border of Texas and the biggest river they had seen so far. It was a challenge, both physical and psychological.

Most of the time, the Red – like the other rivers flowing east across the Plains – was quiet and shallow. But in the mountains to the west, unseen storms could send flash floods down these channels; a river six inches deep could rise to twenty-five feet in a few hours' time. At the Red River Station on the Texas side of the Chisholm Trail ford, the cottonwood trees on the riverbanks all had tangles of driftwood high in their branches, which served as the high-water marks of floods gone by. A more grisly reminder of this danger appeared near the station: rough graves of men who had been killed in past crossings.

Few cowboys were comfortable in deep water, and many couldn't swim at all. They knew their ponies were strong swimmers, and that they wouldn't drown if they clung to their saddles and let the horse take them across, but they hated the whole process. To make matters worse, while most cows were proud and fearless swimmers, there were a dozen ways they could get into trouble while crossing rivers.

If a cow got mired in the quicksand of the river bed, its legs with their pointed hooves sank quickly. And the harder the cow tried to pull out, the faster it sank, until its nostrils vanished beneath the water. It was possible to free a trapped animal, but that meant digging around each leg, folding the leg at the knee, and trussing the leg in that position. Then, with four or five horses pulling on ropes around the cow's horns, it could be pulled out. An alternate method used a wheel of the chuck wagon as a capstan, with the rope wound around the hub. But if the cow's leg got untied and crosswise in the quicksand, it could literally be yanked off; then there was no remedy but to shoot the cow.

Cows in deep water might panic and start swimming in a milling circle, jostling each other and risking drowning in a turbulent jumble of heads, hooves, and horns. In a seemingly endless series of floods on the Red River in the spring of 1871, so many trail herds were waiting to cross that 60,000 head of cattle were backed up on the Texas side.

Arnett and his crew reached the river at a time when it was low and fordable, but it still gave them trouble. Midway through the crossing, with everything going well, Manuel Garcia stopped his chuck wagon to fill the water barrel. As soon as it stopped moving, the wagon sank to its axles in quicksand. Trying to yank it out, Garcia's two oxen wrenched the wagon tongue off. The cowboys cut a hefty cottonwood branch, waded out to the wagon, and lashed it to the frame as a substitute wagon tongue. Then they borrowed two more yoke of oxen from other crews waiting to cross, and the six animals together heaved the wagon out of the quicksand and across the river.

But that victory set up the psychological challenge posed by the Red River. The men had now left the state of Texas and entered what was called The Nations, or Indian Territory, in what is now Oklahoma. It had been settled by Cherokees, Chickasaws, Choctaws, Creeks, and Seminoles - most of them driven by the government from their lands in the East. And it was periodically visited by several of the fiercest and most notorious warrior tribes of the West, including the Comanches and Kiowas.

This was fairly daunting to Fletcher and his fellow

cowboys, whose knowledge of Native Americans was measured by whatever they had read of James Fenimore Cooper's novels. Most of them had seen or heard of trailside mounds with laconic epitaphs: "Killed by Indians." And they were uneasily conscious of the fact that they were about to cross 300 miles of wild and lawless land that belonged to people they thought of as savages, who had no reason to love white men.

These cowboys knew, too, that the worst of the fighting with Indians was over. But only Arnett and the few older hands had first-hand experience of this country, and they all knew that Indians still rustled cattle. The Comanches, in particular, often crept up on a trail herd at night, then stood up and waved blankets to stampede the animals so they could round up a few strays before the cowboys found them.

The T L crew readied their guns, which before now had all been stowed in the chuck wagon. Fletcher stuck his Winchester carbine rifle into the scabbard on his saddle, and the other cowboys strapped on their six-shooters and polished them. "We marched on now, armed to the teeth for savage foes and wild animals," Fletcher wrote.

For weeks, however, they saw no Indians, and spent dozens of bullets in target practice at rabbits and rattlesnakes. It wasn't until the herd had crossed the South Canadian River - almost halfway through Indian Territory - that a band of braves showed up on their ponies, looking exactly as advertised. Fletcher listened anxiously as one of them approached.

But the Indians had come just to beg for a handout of beef. They pleaded, in broken English, that their women and children were hungry. All this seemed a far cry from the noble dignity of Fenimore Cooper's fictional Chingachgook, the last of the Mohicans.

Indeed, this was the dominant tone of cattlemen's relations with the tribes by the end of the 1870s. What the Indians wanted was money, horses, or cattle, by whatever means they could be had. On the old Shawnee Trail, established earlier to link Texas with St. Louis and Kansas City in Missouri, the Cherokees charged a toll of ten cents a head for cattle crossing Indian Territory. To collect it, they set up a police patrol called the Cherokee Light Horse. Farther west, the Comanches sometimes mounted a fearsome mass charge at a trail herd to drive away the cowboys, and then begin butchering and feasting. But most Indians by now were reduced to simple begging, and most trail bosses were willing to buy them off with a steer now and then – preferably a straggler or weakling that probably wouldn't make it to the end of the drive anyway.

As one trail boss reported to his owner, "We struck Indians by the thousands [but] managed to keep peace by giving them a beef every day."

That day they met the Indians, the T L crew had no one else's strays to dispense with. But Arnett found a steer for the Indians and lent them pistols to kill it. They promptly devoured it, with the flesh still twitching and the blood running down their chins. After this performance, Fletcher somewhat sheepishly stowed his Winchester back in the chuck wagon, and the other cowboys put their pistols away, too.

For the T L crew, the passage through Indian Territory after that was mainly a majestic, hypnotic panorama of brown, seared grass, stretching for mile after undulating mile. Dust rose in choking clouds, with more clouds to be seen ahead and behind from other herds on the trail. The cowboys could hear only the ceaseless wind, the clicking of the cows' ankle joints, the thudding of hooves and the occasional clatter of horns accidentally colliding. Now and then, a cow would turn back against the line of march and search, bawling and anxious, for her lost calf.

Off to one side of the herd, all the spare mounts of the remuda walked and grazed under the care of the wrangler, Carteman Garcia. Two or sometimes three times a day, he brought them into jury-rigged rope corrals around the chuck wagon so the men could choose fresh horses. These cow ponies were agile and tough enough to live on water and prairie grass, but they would fall apart quickly if they had to endure more than four or five hours a day of hard riding. So each man got a fresh horse each morning and afternoon, with a third for the night guard. On a hard day, he might need even more. The remuda had enough ponies to give them three days' rest between work stints, but some tough favorites worked more often and seemed to enjoy it.

Arnett's first concern was to drive the herd gently, to make the cattle gain weight on the trail – or at the very least, not to lose it. "Your profit depends on moving them along quiet and easy," one boss explained. "You've no idea how easy it is to knock a dollar off a beef." But these longhorns were almost ideally suited to trail life. Adapting to centuries of life in the wild, they had long legs, hard hooves, great tolerance for heat and cold, and a lot of stamina; and they could go for days, if necessary, without water.

(What longhorns didn't have was tender meat. But perhaps surprisingly, that wasn't enormously important. Early Americans preferred pork to beef. The market for cattle was built around their hides and the tallow that could be rendered from their fat and made into candles, the dominant source of home lighting before kerosene lamps.)

The cattle, simply put, had to be fat.

So the cowboys worked to hold back lead steers

that moved too fast, at the same time they were nudging along the laggards and weaklings in the drag. As one old cowhand put it, "Folks didn't really drive cattle – they moved 'em."

Scouting water on the Great Plains was a major part of the trail boss's job. It was true that longhorns could go for days without water, and that was sometimes necessary. But they would be happier and eat better if well-watered. Bosses also learned to use the cows' talent for sensing water. Some drovers preferred to choose bedding grounds near water, to help move the herd along toward the end of the day when they sniffed water near. Others liked to water the cattle lavishly at noon and bed them on high ground, where the beeves wouldn't be tempted to stray by sniffing a watering hole nearby.

On this barren-looking plain, along the well-trodden Chisholm Trail with its dozens of passing herds, there was a surprising amount of wood for Manuel Garcia's three daily cooking fires. Every river and creek the herd crossed was lined with brush and cottonwood trees. The cook and the wrangler gathered sticks and broken limbs, tossing them into a cowhide slung under the wagon. In even drier country farther north, there were plenty of dried cow or buffalo chips, which were called "prairie coal"; with a bit of bacon rind for kindling, they would give a steady, hot flame. The only drawback: They had to be gathered cautiously, with gloved hands, since nearly every one came with a scorpion underneath.

In this stretch of Indian Territory, as detailed in Baylis Fletcher's memoir, the work was constant. Before the drive began back in Texas, the cowboys had indulged in practical jokes on each other; once, when Joe Felder fell asleep beside a river where the crew had seen alligators, Manuel Garcia threw a log into the river and yelled, "Alligator!" Startled awake, Felder tried to get to his feet and slipped into the water beside the log, screaming for help. His friends lassoed him and dragged him out, to be endlessly hazed as the man terrified of a log. But here, there was no time or inclination for fun and games.

The night routine of the camp was unchanged. Supper – more beans and bacon – was followed by time around the campfire, telling yarns, singing, or simply sitting and smoking in slumped exhaustion. On a given night, one cowboy might be playing a harmonica; two more could be arguing inconclusively over whether the face on the moon was male or female. A third might be working over a new verse for "The Old Chisholm Trail," the most popular of all night-guard songs:

> O a ten dollar hoss and a forty-dollar saddle
> And I'm goin' to punch in Texas cattle

> I woke up one morning on the old
> Chisholm Trail

Rope in my hand and a cow by the tail

Coma ti yi youpy, youpy yea, youpy yea
Coma ti yi youp, youpy yea . . .

The light began to fail at about 8:00, signaling the start of the night's first two-hour watch. The two cowboys assigned to it would begin to bed down the cattle. They rode slow, diminishing circles around the grazing longhorns, bunching them closer together. After most of the beeves were lying down, one of the two riders reversed course. The men continued circling the resting herd in opposite directions, singing slow, quiet songs to keep the cattle calm.

Some of the songs were traditional lullabies or popular tunes; others were made up, on the spot or around the campfire, with interminable new verses like "The Old Chisholm Trail." Fletcher favored Presbyterian hymns, which he said had a quieting effect on the animals. A cowboy from another trail herd liked to play his fiddle to the cattle, and he claimed that his two favorite tunes, "Dinah Had a Wooden Leg" and "The Unfortunate Pup," were especially tranquilizing.

If he wasn't on the first watch, Fletcher used this time to walk out to the remuda to pick out a horse for his own guard duty later in the night. Fletcher also took along a spare horse, which he hobbled - tying its front legs close together with a rawhide cord so it wouldn't wander far. Then he joined the men around the campfire, but it wasn't long before he nestled into his bedroll and fell asleep. What with guard duty and an early start in the morning, none of the men ever got more than six hours of sleep.

At midnight, a cowboy coming off the second watch woke Fletcher up with a quiet word. It was strictly against the code to shake or even touch a sleeper, who might be alarmed and strike out or even shoot at the intruder. Fletcher stretched, put on the pants that had been rolled up for his pillow, and walked out to mount his favorite horse, Happy Jack, for his shift.

The pony had all the traits that made a good night horse. It was quiet and self-possessed, not inclined to take fright and shy at shadows or startling noises. Happy Jack had eyes much sharper than a day horse needed and could pick through brush and gullies in the pitch darkness, or gallop at night without stepping into a prairie-dog hole and breaking a leg. Most important, the horse could help control cattle stampeding in the dark – which was when stampedes most often happened.

Fletcher knew just by glancing at the stars that he had been roused right on time, at midnight. Few cowboys had watches, and most relied on the sun and stars to tell the time; on cloudy nights, they could count on their horses to tell them when the shift was done. A Texas night horse named Old Sid was famous for refusing to work for more than two hours. If his rider for some reason had to stay on guard longer than that, the cowboy had to ride into camp, dismount, and wait two minutes or so before riding out again. Then Old Sid was persuaded that the right thing had been done and would consent to work again.

Even though the T L herd hadn't stampeded since the first weeks on the trail, the possibility that the cattle might bolt was ever-present for Fletcher and his fellow night guards. Any of a thousand things could touch off a stampede – a coyote's bark, a startled jack rabbit, a bolt of lightning or the rattle of thunder, even the flare of a cowboy's match as he lit a cigarette.

The cost of a stampede could be enormous. At the very least, even if the cattle were all rounded up, they lost thousands of collective pounds of fat in the running. And it could be much worse. One herd was spooked when a shred of tobacco from a cowboy's pouch blew into a steer's eye; by the time they were rounded up, 400 beeves were lost and two men had died.

In full run, the charging herd normally didn't hurt the men. The river of cattle tended to split around a fallen rider – a graciousness nobody deliberately chose to test. But a cowboy trying to turn the stampede could be vulnerable to being gored or getting swept off the saddle by a horn and falling under the hooves. When the cattle had turned and were milling in their dense pack, riders who got trapped in the whirlpool were also in peril. In one stampede near the Blue River in Nebraska, all that was found of a cowboy downed in the mill was his gun butt. Everything else had been shredded and trampled into the sod.

Some cattlemen, like the entrepreneur Joseph McCoy of Abilene, were convinced that many stampedes were caused by "troublemakers" among the herd – steers that he said "would rather run than eat, anytime." McCoy wrote: "The stampeders may be seen close together at all times, as if consulting how to raise Cain and get off with a burst of speed." He argued that it would save money for a trail boss "to shoot down a squad of these vicious stampeders." In practice, however, more cowboys calmed those prone to run by sewing their eyelids shut; thus temporarily blinded, they would have to stick closely to other cattle to find food and water. By the time the thread rotted and the animals could see again, they seemed to have learned their lesson.

Stampedes and other perils always plagued the cowboy, and most had their own methods or subscribed to some other sage advice for dealing with those problems. But before 1879, getting good information – on everything from weather to Indian attacks – was troublesome.

By the time Baylis Fletcher made his first cattle

drive, the Chisholm Trail was heavily traveled, and news flowed up and down it with surprising efficiency. As the herds plodded north, freighters driving heavy wagons south brought word of weather and events ahead. When a cowboy from the herd in front dropped back to look for strays or a lost horse, he sometimes traded gossip with Arnett and his men. And by this time, the Kansas Pacific Railway was publishing a map and trail guide to the Chisholm, in an effort to attract traffic to its railhead at Dodge City. One entry, for instance, described the terrain along the Cimarron River, which the T L herd was about to cross for the first of four times.

Unfortunately, the trail guide wasn't infallible. Until recently, the Chisholm Trail had taken an easier route through Kansas to Dodge City, but homesteaders rebelling at the passing herds had forced a detour to the west that wound back and forth with the river. What the trail guide didn't say was that the second Cimarron crossing was so fouled by alkali that a long drink of that water could easily kill a cow.

To make matters worse, trail boss Arnett had been badly hurt when his horse fell on him, nearly crushing his leg. He had to spend a week riding in an improvised bunk on the chuck wagon, and the crew was in disarray without his leadership, bickering as rivals tried to assume authority. Luckily, just as they reached the Cimarron juncture, a rider named Bud Armstrong arrived. He carried a letter from boss Tom Snyder, authorizing Armstrong to guide the herd through this treacherous section of the trail.

Armstrong said more than a hundred cattle in a single outfit had died of alkali poisoning at the second Cimarron River crossing. Since it was all but impossible to prevent the T L herd from drinking as they crossed the river, there was only one solution: To stampede the herd on purpose through the crossing. That would be as risky as a stampede always was, and also a novelty; the herd hadn't stampeded at all since those first weeks in Texas, and this could risk getting the longhorns back into the habit. But there was no choice.

Arnett was glad to give Armstrong full authority, and after the chaos caused by their rivalries, the men were equally glad to defer to him. So all the way up to the riverbank, the cowboys worked together to bunch the cattle into a compact mass and keep them under a tight hold; then, just as the lead steer reached the water, the men yelled, flapped their hats and slickers, and spooked the herd into a frenzied run right across the riverbed. Far sooner than usual in a stampede, the longhorns calmed down and tried to double back for a drink. The vastly outnumbered cowboys had to fight hard all night and into the next day to prevent scattered bunches of cattle from reaching the river. But they finally got the herd together and moving north again, unpoisoned. The next day, they found ample fresh water in a tributary, Buffalo Creek, with abundant grass close by. They decided to rest the herd there for a day.

The stay was extended when Tom Snyder himself arrived, in a carriage from Dodge City, to tell the crew that he had sold 300 beeves to be fed to Indians on a nearby reservation. Four cowboys were sent off to deliver those cattle, and Snyder returned to Dodge. Since Arnett was now well enough to ride, Snyder took Armstrong with him. For the crew, trail life returned to normal.

For Baylis Fletcher, however, there was a memorable scare. While the four men were away delivering the reservation cattle, the remaining crew had to take night guard duty one man at a time. Riding guard alone was dangerous. One particular night, the risks seemed greater after Arnett refused to give a beef to some insolent Cheyennes, who had gone away disgruntled. During his solo shift that night, Fletcher carried a borrowed six-gun. When a wolf howled in the darkness, he thought of tales he had heard about Indians signaling attacks with animal noises. More wolves howled, and came closer.

Fletcher clutched his revolver. Finally he saw something that seemed to be slinking near the herd. "I made a dash for it and found that it was a real wolf," he wrote, "after which I fired several shots, greatly accelerating its flight. After that, I felt more secure. The wolves were real, and I had nothing to fear from them."

Meanwhile, Arnett's luck held. At the end of June, the T L herd made its last crossing of the Cimarron River into the state of Kansas. There had been no more stampedes or poisoned water, and the animals were in good shape. Now, they were again in settled territory, signified by a line of buffalo skulls, placed at half-mile intervals along the Kansas side of the river. This line marked the new detour of the Chisholm Trail, leading to the railhead at Dodge City. (Homesteaders along the old route had rebelled at the damage done to their pastures by the endless herds, and the Kansas government had banned all Texas cattle from the east central part of the state.)

There was only one problem with the new cutoff to Dodge City, but it was a real hurdle: a stretch of a hundred miles, from the Cimarron to the Arkansas River, with hardly any water along the way. At its usual speed, the herd could cross that distance in eight days. But by that time, the cattle might be dying or dead; even sooner, parched cows could panic if their calves seemed to be in trouble. Arnett decided to double the pace and reach the Arkansas in four days. The cowboys let the cattle drink their fill and set out at dawn. Marching steadily, grazing through the midday heat, and plodding on again until after dark, the tired cattle were visibly skinnier every day.

The risks were real. After three or four days without water, cattle could go blind. They could also become unmanageable and insist on turning back to the last water they could remember, even if they died before reaching it. But once again, the cowboys' luck held. After the third day of the long trek, a providential rain squall drenched the prairie and left puddles along the trail for the herd to lap up. It was just enough that when the cattle reached the Arkansas River, they were able to avoid the frenzied overdrinking that could have overwhelmed their bodies and killed them.

That danger was real, too. The most notorious dry trail in the West was the one that the famous Texas owner Charlie Goodnight first drove a herd across – eighty barren, blast-furnace miles from the Concho River in west Texas to the Pecos in New Mexico. The only way to make it was to water the cattle at the Concho in the morning and push straight through, reaching the Pecos at midnight, with the cows eating and drinking nothing and the men living on black coffee. Some cowboys had to rub tobacco juice in their eyes to stay awake on that drive, and ten miles from the end, when the cattle smelled the Pecos, the men had to summon the energy to keep them from stampeding to the river. Some steers bolted over the bank and killed themselves anyway, while others got trampled to death; many that made it to the stream overdrank and died.

But most of the herd had the instinctive wisdom to wade into the water, moaning, and stand submerged to their shoulders for half an hour before drinking anything. Then they lapped up a little, stood another hour before drinking again, and then ambled out to graze. Three centuries of longhorn survival heredity saved them.

As was customary after a dry drive, Arnett let his herd rest for a couple of days, grazing and watering often, in a pasture just across the Arkansas River. It was within plain sight of Dodge City, a cow town on the Union Pacific Railroad.

With its saloons, dance halls, and brothels, Dodge City was a notorious mecca for cowboys – the "beautiful, bibulous Babylon of the trail," according to a romanticizing chronicler of the day. Bibulous, at least, it was. But Arnett had been schooled in his boss Snyder's puritanical ways. He allowed his crew only a few hours in town, and then only in daylight, when the dance halls were closed and the women sleeping.

On July 6, the cowboys gathered the herd for the last 380 miles of their long drive, northwest through Kansas and Nebraska into Wyoming.

The first notable sight on the road out of Dodge was the carcass of a horse, killed by lightning, with the grave of its rider nearby. It was another reminder of the T L luck: the herd and its crew had been spared the worst of the spectacular electric storms of the Western Plains, probably the second most frequent cause of death of cowboys on the trail. (A cowboy in Kansas recalled lightning that "would hit the side of those hills and gouge out great holes in the earth like a bomb had struck them, and it killed seven or eight cattle in the herd back of us.")

There was no way to avoid lightning; all a cowboy could do was pray. Though some cowboys caught in electric storms tried to shuck anything made of metal – from spurs and belt buckles to knives and six-guns – and stash it somewhere far enough away to be safe. (Others took care to avoid cursing while a storm was raging, so as not to tempt divine wrath.)

The T L crew did ride through some thunder squalls in July, but took no damage. Their only problem was with the settlers along the trail, who often harassed the herd and refused to let it graze in local pastures. But before they left Kansas, they had a last scare – one that rattled their nerves before, paradoxically, it eased their way to the border.

One day near the town of Oberlin, on the Sappa River, the trail suddenly filled with settlers, hurrying past the herd with wagonloads of their children and possessions. They were heading for the safety of towns, they said, because Comanches were on the warpath and had scalped several people. The T L crew couldn't leave their cattle, but they agreed to sleep that night hidden in a grove of trees, away from the cattle and the chuck wagon. They passed an uneasy, if uneventful, night that way.

The next morning, Fletcher and his fellow cowboys were overtaken by a herd of horses, being driven to Nebraska. "See any Indians?" this group's trail boss asked the T L riders. When they said no, he laughed. "We are the only Indians in western Kansas," he said. The warlike Comanches were imaginary, his solution to the nuisance of the settlers: He had depopulated the country by spreading the rumor of the raid, and now had open grazing all the way to the border. The T L cowboys were chagrined at being fooled by the ruse, but grateful to share the benefits as they followed the horses north and west.

Nebraska proved an easy march, up the lush valley of the Platte River leading into Wyoming. The terrain rose to 4,000 feet above sea level, and the air turned cooler even though the noon sun was still fierce. For men used to Texas conditions, the nights were almost too cold for comfort. Just more than a hundred miles from the end of their journey, they turned out of the Platte Valley into an old Mormon trail along Lodgepole Creek.

Fletcher was struck by the terrible relics of the Mormon pioneers' desperate journey into Utah. Here were broken fragments of the handcarts they pushed, in lieu of the horse-drawn wagons they couldn't afford. Here were graves of Mormons who died from the fierce blizzards, the Indian attacks, and the terrible ailments of the plains. It had been twenty-three years since that pilgrimage, and the Latter-Day Saints were prospering now in their valley on the Great Salt Lake.

The valley of Lodgepole Creek narrowed to a canyon before the herd crossed into Wyoming at a town called Pine Bluffs. Now, the crew had less than forty miles to go: a local foreman for the buyers, the Swan Brothers Cattle Company, told Arnett to turn over the cattle at a ranch twenty miles north of Cheyenne.

On the morning of August 12, 1879, the crew found itself on a great plateau, 6,000 feet high, with the snow-tipped Rocky Mountains gleaming a hundred miles farther west. It was the grandest sight Fletcher had ever seen. "I feasted my eyes for several days on the backbone of America," he wrote.

Three days later, the drive ended at the Swan Brothers pasture, and suddenly the whole enterprise fell apart. Another company bought the remuda, including Happy Jack, and someone else bought the chuck wagon and incidental gear. Everything that had held the T L crew together was dissipating. Cashing in a letter of credit on a bank in Cheyenne, Arnett gave each cowboy his pay – $100, more or less, depending on old obligations and advances taken during the drive.

In Cheyenne, the cowboys splurged on baths, shaves,

haircuts and new clothing; the transformation was so great that they hardly recognized each other when they met on the streets. Some, freed from Arnett's straitlaced orders, hit the saloons and dance halls; the prudent ones bought their tickets home before getting into card games.

Led by Arnett, some of the cowboys took rooms at Dodge's Metropolitan Hotel. At breakfast the next day, a black man had the temerity to take a seat at a table next to theirs. "It had been only fourteen years since the close of the Civil War, and race prejudice was still strong," Fletcher explained. "Mr. Arnett, unfortunately, did not take time to protest. He merely arose and smashed his chair over the head of the Negro." The trail boss was arrested and "heavily fined," Fletcher wrote.

But Arnett was soon released, and with most of the crew, he boarded a train to Texas.

Baylis Fletcher, captivated by Wyoming, hired on for a short local cattle drive in the high country. After his four-month trek over a distance one-third the span of the United States, this was an easy ride through the hills. Then one day, without thinking much about it, he went to the Union Pacific station and bought a ticket to Texas.

His great adventure had ended.

6
COW TOWNS
THE "SODOMS OF THE PLAINS"

In the annals of the Old West, the long drive towns were almost as legendary as the cowboys themselves. These places had two purposes – to load cattle on trains and ship them to market, and to relieve cowboys as quickly as possible of the pay they had earned on their long drives from Texas.

The first goal was achieved by erecting a sturdy complex of corrals for the cattle, with huge scales capable of weighing twenty beeves at a time and chutes through which the animals could be prodded and cajoled to climb into the waiting boxcars.

The second target was hit with a judicious mix of strong drink, overpriced merchandise, unscrupulous gambling games, and prostitutes.

These "soiled doves," as the newspapers called prostitutes, had hard faces, raucous laughs, and all-too-apt nicknames: Cross-Eyed Sue, Hambone Nelly, The Galloping Cow, Scarface Jane and Squirrel-Tooth Mary.

The cowboys played their own part with self-conscious relish. On the trail and back at the ranch, they followed the rules and generally behaved with courage, good judgment and a firm adherence to their strict code of honor. But in the cow towns, they were free to act out and reinforce their image as hard-drinking, free-spending carousers. And most of them grabbed the opportunity with a whooping, pistol-firing vengeance.

"Well-mounted and full of their favorite beverage," as Daniel Wilder wrote in *The Annals of Kansas* in 1886, "the cowboys will dash through the principal streets of a town, yelling like Comanches. This they call 'cleaning out a town.'"

Overgrown boys on their first trail drive tried to match the older men drink for drink. They paid wildly inflated prices for hats, boots and clothing to replace the clothes worn out on the long drive. They gawked at freak shows and danced wild frontier dances with bar girls, who were likely to wind up with whatever money the cowboys had left at the end of their stay in town.

As the ballad *The Cowboy's Lament* set the order

of business, "'Twas first to the cardhouse and then down to Maisie's." But in reality, the cowboy's first stop in town was to get a bath. He was desperate to feel clean again after months of wearing the same clothes, sleeping in his pungent bedroll, and being washed only by the muddy water of river fords. Even then, he needed a shave and a haircut before he would be welcomed by either the saloon-cardhouse or the girls at Maisie's. But the newspapers and dime novels had already painted a fanciful worldwide portrait of the cowboy of the American West - and the vast majority of the hands were more than ready to reinforce and burnish that image.

Some trail bosses, like George Arnett, were spoilsports who restricted their cowhands to daytime visits to limit their temptations. And a few of the men barely got started on a spree before being recalled for an emergency. "I had paid $1.25 for a haircut and a shave," wrote one cowboy, "and I had to go back to the herd and stand guard all night during a severe storm."

The cow towns were unique in the history of America – short-lived boom towns as wide-open as the mining camps of the 'Forty-Niner gold rush or the later Klondike, but at the intersection of the Western Plains with the civilization represented by the railroad. For a brief two decades after the Civil War, the towns could spring up anywhere a trail from Texas crossed one of the tracks being pushed ever farther west. Within weeks, the corrals and loading chutes were constructed; enterprising saloon-keepers threw up their unpainted, false-front establishments; and a hotel was built for the drovers to reach their deals with the buyers. Haberdashers and suppliers operated from shacks or even tents. Some of the saloons quickly expanded into gambling and dance halls; and a red-light district was set aside for the outright brothels.

A dozen or more such cow towns flourished before, just as suddenly, they died out. But the business model for the whole enterprise sprang from the head of one man: Joseph Geiting McCoy. He was the scion of an Illinois family that had grown rich in the cattle trade, and the founding father of perhaps the grandest cow town of them all: Abilene, Kansas.

McCoy got the first gleam of his idea when a friend, recently back from the Civil War, told him about the millions of longhorns roaming the plains of Texas - and now being rounded up and branded.

As the cattle barons of Texas were getting ready to drive their herds to market, McCoy studied the maps of the western states. Astutely, he recognized that most cattle drives from Texas would pass through Kansas, the most easily navigable spot on the map, to reach the railroad tracks.

The western end of the Union Pacific Railroad had reached Salina, Kansas, in the spring of 1867, when McCoy boarded a train to explore the possibilities there. On the way, the train stopped for an hour while a bridge was being repaired.

McCoy got off and found himself in the hamlet of Abilene. Named from a passage in the Bible, Abilene meant "city of the plains." But, when McCoy first saw this Abilene, it was no city. He described it as "a small, dead place, consisting of about one dozen log huts" and not many more inhabitants. A man named Tim Hersey, who claimed to be the founding father, served meals to stagecoach passengers in his cabin, and Josiah Jones ran a dismally quiet saloon.

McCoy's opinion of Salina, when he got there, wasn't much higher - and land prices were too high in nearby Junction City. But on reflection, Abilene had some advantages that were not, at first, obvious. It was west of the territory that had been settled by farmers, who would resist having herds driven over their land, and it was already served by the railroad. Even better, there was no competition for land or rights in the village's bleak vicinity. It didn't matter that Abilene had no facilities for handling cattle; McCoy decided that this would be the place.

There was a problem with the whole idea: the cattle disease then known as Texas fever, a tick-borne parasitic infection fatal to most cattle. Longhorns weren't bothered by it, but they could transmit the disease. Thus, Kansas had established a quarantine zone banning cattle from Texas. Abilene was within the quarantine zone. But McCoy deftly sidestepped this issue by calling on the governor, and getting his assurance that the ban wouldn't be enforced.

Next, he bought 250 acres in and near Abilene. He also got the Union Pacific to promise to carry cattle at $5 a carload all the way to Chicago. The railroad also promised to install switches and sidings for the loading operation – testimony to McCoy's persuasive powers, since otherwise there was no sign of cattle to be shipped anywhere near Abilene.

To make sure there would be some, McCoy sent another cattle dealer, W. W. Sugg, 200 miles south into Indian Territory to find drovers and point them toward Abilene. He also recruited family and friends to promote Abilene in the East and enlist like-minded speculators as partners in the endeavor.

In less than two months, Abilene was transformed.

Dipping into his family funds, McCoy ordered lumber from Missouri to build a set of stock pens stout enough to hold 3,000 rambunctious Texas Longhorns. He installed a ten-ton scale to weigh the cattle in batches of twenty. He built an office, a barn, a livery stable, and an eighty-room hotel that he called the Drovers' Cottage. And he spread the word to enterprising retailers, saloon-keepers and gamblers that cowboys with money would soon be at hand.

Sure enough, one day in August 1867, before the last touches were applied to the new facilities, the longhorns began to arrive. By September 5, twenty carloads had rolled off to Chicago. That count rose to 1,000 by November, when the first Abilene season ended. Over its five-year career as a cow town, more than a million cattle would pass through.

The *New York Tribune* spread the news, reporting breathlessly that McCoy's operation could "load a train of forty cars in two hours." The publicity, along with McCoy's promotion, drew dozens of sharpies angling to cash in on the bonanza. Before long, two retailers, according to the *Tribune*, had "extemporized a store out of an empty cornbin . . . selling the goods they receive from Fort Leavenworth, at from 150 to 200 percent profit, almost as fast as they can take them from the boxes."

But as the next season's drives were beginning, McCoy's triumph threatened to collapse. Rumors spread that the longhorns were bringing an epidemic of Texas fever that would decimate Kansas's cattle, and prospective buyers were no longer planning to come to Abilene. McCoy's response would have impressed even P.T. Barnum: an extravaganza of showmanship designed not to refute the rumors, but to bury them in an avalanche of ballyhoo.

He began by hiring some cowboys to scout for buffalo on the prairie west of Abilene. They caught several, including a bull that weighed more than a ton. With his cowboys, the buffalo, and some elk and wild horses, McCoy headed for St. Louis and Chicago to put on one of the first prototypes of the Wild West shows later made famous by Buffalo Bill Cody. His cowboys, in chaps, bandannas and spurs, were reinforced by Mexican *vaqueros* in red sashes and black velvet trousers. All of them dazzled the crowds as they roped, rode, and wrestled the animals to the ground. The whole show was built around Abilene and the promise of the fat beeves to be found there, and somehow the specter of Texas fever grew less scary.

At the climax of the show in both cities, McCoy invited everyone in the house to come to Abilene for a buffalo hunt. Those who accepted the invitation were treated to a hunt and then taken to the stockyards, where thousands of Texas longhorns were waiting – all seemingly healthy and well-fed - to be bid on. McCoy's scheme worked, and when the 1868 season ended, Abilene was the West's leading shipper of cattle. In 1869, fully 150,000 longhorns passed through Abilene to market.

By 1870, the onetime settlement of a dozen log cabins was famous all over America as the prototypical cattle town. At its heart were the stockyards, fragrant and noisy, with beeves pawing the ground, bawling, and clashing their horns together as they waited to be loaded into boxcars.

Around the corner from the stockyards was one of

the town's showplaces, the Drovers' Cottage - three stories high and splendid in yellow paint, green trim and Venetian blinds. This was a mecca where drovers and buyers could make their handshake deals in hushed lounges. The dining room was said to rival the best Eastern restaurants, and behind the hotel was a stable that could house a hundred horses and fifty carriages. Across the railroad tracks and within sight of the stockyards was another showplace, the home that McCoy had built for his family.

Much of the heart of Abilene, however, was a three-block stretch of Texas Street devoted to the town's second business: separating cowboys from the money they earned on the long trail. Abileners were good at it. "I had to sow my wild oats," one cowboy recalled about his visit to Abilene, "and I regret to say that I also sowed all the money I made right along with the oats."

Not far from the Drovers' Cottage was the town's most elegant saloon, the original Alamo, with swinging doors made of glass instead of wood and paintings of nude women on the walls. Nuggets and gold dust lay on the green baize gambling tables, and the mirrors reflected polished brass fixtures, pyramids of glasses, and dozens of bottles of whiskey, brandy and rum. Eight lesser saloons sat along the street, typified by the Bull's Head with the huge red bull on its signboard. All were places where a cowboy on a spree could gamble, drink, and find a woman.

Also along Texas Street were the retailers, highlighted by Henry H. Hazlett's Farmers and Drovers Supply Store, Jake Karatofsky's gents' furnishings emporium, and Thomas C. McInerney's custom bootmaking shop. There were hardware stores, blacksmith shops, and boarding houses, where the cowboys could take baths and sleep on clean sheets. And there was a photography studio, where a cowboy could pose in his new finery for a trophy to take back to Texas.

Just outside of town, at a distance that varied over time with the respectable citizens' degree of outrage, was the red-light district. It was known as the Devil's Addition, or sometimes McCoy's Addition, since it was McCoy, as Abilene's leading spirit, who had taken the lead in moving the soiled doves outside the town's official limits. Here women (also referred to as *nymphs du prairie*, calico queens and painted cats) plied their sex trade in unpainted shacks, lean-tos and sometimes tents. And here, as a lumber dealer in town lamented, "Money and whiskey flowed like water downhill, and youth and beauty and womanhood and manhood were wrecked and damned in that valley of perdition."

But it was impossible to confine the women to their assigned place. They circulated freely in the saloons and dance halls, and were known to skinny-dip with their customers in the Smoky Hill River that ran right through Abilene.

No one even tried to enforce the rudimentary rules. For its first three seasons as a cow town, Abilene had no government or law enforcement mechanism. When the drovers started arriving, the citizens of nearby towns complained that "Hell is now in session." The newspaper of a nearby small town reported in characteristic hyperbole: "Murder, lust, highway robbery, and whores run the city day and night. Seventeen souls snatched from this earth, seventeen souls taken in their sins, ushered before their God without a moment's warning, all of this done at our county seat."

Abilene, though, was rapidly changing. The more respectable citizens weren't too keen on the town's six-month seasonal business of gambling and prostitution. In addition, more and more farmers settled the surrounding countryside - and by 1870, their presence was drawing preachers, teachers, blacksmiths, saddlers, grocers, dry-goods and clothing merchants, doctors, dentists, and inevitably lawyers. Abilene now boasted a jewelry store, two churches, a furniture store, and a newspaper, *The Abilene Chronicle*. Children were being brought to Abilene, and more were being born; to accommodate them, a stone schoolhouse was being built on the edge of town.

The town's businessmen, who originally competed for the trade of the free-spending cattlemen passing through, slowly learned that the local trade was more dependable - and more lucrative in the long run.

Predictably, the respectable townsfolk wanted change. One of McCoy's cronies, T.C. Henry, who had come to town to join the predators, had opened a real estate office that now sold ten to fifteen farms a day. Henry had built himself another showplace home, and he now saw that Abilene's real future lay not in the cattle trade but in commercial development. He became a leader in the revolt against wide-open raffishness, as well as the movement to incorporate the town, and eventually, he wrote Abilene's first ordinances to bring law and order.

After the county government granted his petition to incorporate Abilene and allow it to elect town officials, Henry became its interim mayor. He soon signed ordinances banning firearms, fining prostitution, and requiring licenses for saloon-keeping and gambling. The ordinances were posted on billboards along the town roads, where jeering cowboys initially shot them full of holes.

Henry then set out to hire a marshal. How could you enforce the law without a lawman? You couldn't. But a good man, as he found out, was surprisingly hard to find.

The first two candidates for the job left town - too rowdy, they discerned. But then Henry found

Thomas James Smith, a onetime New York policeman who had won the nickname "Bear River Tom" for helping to quell a bloody riot at Bear River, Wyoming, while bleeding from a severe gunshot wound.

Smith was a redhead with an impressive physical stature, a low voice, and steady, gray-blue eyes. Because he seldom had the need to draw it, his gun was seen only as a bulge in his coat. His first challenge came on a Saturday night soon after he took the job, when Big Hank, a well-known desperado, swaggered into town with a gun on his hip and refused to give it up when the marshal demanded it. Smith decked him with one punch to the jaw, confiscated the pistol, and ordered him out of town. To the amazement of all the spectators, Big Hank slunk away.

Word of that got around in a flash, and an even tougher character named Wyoming Frank bet his cronies that he could face down the marshal. On Sunday morning, Frank took a stand on the main street, and when Smith showed up, started flinging abuse at him. Bear River Tom locked eyes with Frank, walked steadily up to him and quietly asked for his gun. Frank started backing away, with the marshal following. Finally, he backed into a saloon, where Smith punched him, threw him to the floor, took away his gun, and ordered him to leave town. Tamely, Wyoming Frank followed Big Hank's example.

In the hushed saloon, its owner was the first to speak. "That was the nerviest act I ever saw," T.C. Henry quoted him later. "You did your duty, and that coward got what he deserved. Here is my gun. I reckon I'll not need it as long as you are marshal." He and his patrons handed Smith their weapons.

From then on, all strangers in Abilene left their guns at a saloon, a hotel or a store, to be claimed again only on their way out of town. The townsfolk were so grateful that they raised Smith's pay from $150 a month to $225, more than twice what a trail boss would make.

Bear River Tom kept the peace for five months. But then, in November 1870, he went out one night to arrest a farmer who was wanted for murder. He caught up to the man at his dugout and easily subdued him. But one of the farmer's friends, also suspected of taking part in the murder, burst from hiding and decapitated the marshal with an axe.

The post went unfilled for five months of the off-season, but in April, as the herds were approaching, Joe McCoy – now Abilene's mayor – found what seemed the perfect new marshal: James Butler (Wild Bill) Hickok. A onetime Union Army scout who may have been the fastest gun in the West, Hickok was said to have killed more white men than any other man on the Frontier. He presided over Abilene from a green baize table at the Alamo, steadily drinking whiskey and playing cards.

Hickok wore his two revolvers as his tools, one on each hip, with their butts facing forward to ease his fast draw – which he could perform either cross-handed or by plucking the pistols out by the trigger guard and twirling them into shooting position.

In large part due to Hickok's formidable reputation, the cattle season of 1871 came and went without any major hitches. Until, that is, one night in October, when the marshal heard a shot on the street outside the Alamo. Running out, he found a crowd of fifty revelers, including a man waving a gun, who claimed he had shot a dog. Wild Bill confronted him and both men fired shots; the drunken gunman fell dead. Then a second policeman, Hickok's deputy Mike Williams, ran out of the darkness. Startled, Wild Bill killed him, too.

The good citizens of Abilene decided that Hickok was all too quick on the draw, and that his brand of enforcement was just another form of lawlessness. He was fired and replaced in December.

But over the winter, Abilene also decided to be freed from the basic cause of its disorder: Both cows and cowboys would have to go. T. C. Henry wrote out a manifesto, which was printed in the *Chronicle* on February 8, 1872, over fifty-two signatures: "We the undersigned members of the Farmers' Protective Association and Officers and Citizens of Dickinson County, Kansas, most respectfully request all who have contemplated driving Texas Cattle to Abilene the coming season to seek some other point for shipment, as the inhabitants of Dickinson will no longer submit to the evils of the trade."

The statement was republished three times and later appeared in several Texas newspapers. Each time, the list of signatures grew until the number reached 366. The drovers of Texas heeded the message. In the 1872 season, they headed for other cattle towns, which had been springing up to compete with Abilene for the growing trade.

The saloon-keepers, gamblers, prostitutes and hangers-on left Abilene, too. So did many legitimate businessmen, who still liked to deal with the open-handed cattlemen and cowboys. A Texas promoter, Moses B. George, bought the grand Drovers' Cottage hotel, had it disassembled and loaded onto a flat car, and shipped it to the up-and-coming cow town of Ellsworth, Kansas, where he reopened it under the same name. Joe McCoy followed the cattle trade, too. Later, he designed the stock pens for the new cow town of Newton, and promoted the operation in Wichita; he ended his career counting cattle for the U.S. Census Bureau.

Abilene settled happily into quiet obscurity. "Business is not as brisk as it used to be during the cattle season," the *Chronicle* editorialized in the summer of 1872, "but the citizens have the satisfaction of knowing that 'Hell is more than sixty miles away.'"

Abilene set the pattern for the dozen or more rival cattle towns that sprang up, flourished, and then were tamed over the span of the cattle drives. These included Ellsworth, Newton, Wichita, Hays City, Ellis, Caldwell, Dodge City, and Ogalalla – all in Kansas or near its border. Thousands of drovers and cowboys from Texas rode into these towns during those two decades to be joined by Easterners, who came to buy the cows, share in the carousing, or profiteer at the cowboys' expense.

All the towns shared the boom-and-bust cycle, but each had its own distinctive life span. Newton, sixty miles south of Abilene, compressed the whole story into a single year, 1871, after the Atchison, Topeka & Santa Fe Railroad reached the town.

A cowboy who passed through Newton on his way to Abilene that May recalled, "A blacksmith shop, a store, and about a dozen dwellings made up this town at the time, but when we came back through the place on our return home thirty days later, it had grown to be quite a large town." Of the buildings, only the railroad depot had plastered walls; the rest were constructed of unpainted boards, and many of them had false fronts jutting into the sky. There were also shacks, converted corn cribs and canvas tents. The first herds arrived to find grass still growing in the streets, and prairie dogs poking their heads through the grass.

There were just two wells in town, but twenty-seven saloons were selling stronger drink at twenty-five cents a glass. The red-light district was called Hide Park, and there, as the rival *Wichita Tribune* reported: "You may see young girls not over sixteen drinking whisky, smoking cigars, cursing, and swearing until one almost loses the respect they should have for the weaker sex. I heard one of their townsmen say that he didn't believe there were a dozen virtuous women in town."

In its brief career as a cow town, Newton never hired any law enforcement. But the gamblers, apparently feeling they needed protection from the men they were cheating, pooled some money to hire guards. The clatter of gunfire in town, one resident complained, "reminded me of a Fourth of July celebration. There was shooting when I got up and when I went to bed." Estimates of casualties that year ran from nine to fifty dead – the latter surely a hyperbolic horror story from a rival for the cattle trade.

This rivalry, which often played out on the pages of the local newspapers, was almost comic – especially between Wichita and Ellsworth. "If the lack of water and short grass are required to the well-being of Texas cattle," sniped The *Wichita City Eagle*, "then Ellsworth is the point." The *Ellsworth Reporter* retorted that everyone knew longhorns tended to be "wild and unruly, and easily stampeded by any degree of annoyance from flies and mosquitoes, which prevail to an alarming extent this year in and around Wichita, and which owe their increased number to the humid and sultry weather experienced there during the spring and summer."

Each town promoted its own attractions and paid influential Texas cattle barons to persuade their friends to bring their herds to its stock pens. Wichita gave actual kickbacks to drovers who brought cattle to town, and its bank offered them loans at interest rates as low as 3 percent, while charging local farmers usurious rates as high as 60 percent. One year, the Wichita city council passed a resolution guaranteeing unimpeded passage to any drover who wanted to take his cows right down the main street.

The railroads also shared in the bonanza, with carload rates for cattle as high as $40 when they had the only track. But they would cut the price to $10 or less in rate wars when another line reached a nearby town.

None of the cow towns, however, neglected their second goal of attracting and catering to cowboys. Some offered unlikely diversions, from bowling alleys to roller-skating rinks. The *Wichita Eagle* busily promoted the town's pony track, promising that cowboys could have a good time while using their knowledge of horseflesh to get rich quick.

On one Saturday afternoon at the races, the paper reported, "More than one thousand men were present, besides five carriages of soiled doves."

But the cow towns all shared an ambience, similar to that depicted in classic Western movies. The weathered, unpainted false fronts of buildings poked into the prairie sky. The sounds and smells of the stockyard hung in the air. The unpaved streets sent up clouds of dust, or turned to quagmires in the rare rainstorms; the sidewalks were made of boards to keep the shoes of the soiled doves clean.

Sooner or later, all the cattle towns were destined to go the way of Abilene, reining in the cowboys and their exploiters alike in the name of law, order, and sober tranquility. "Over the entire scene hovered the stern silence of disapproval that emanated from the cattle town's handful of respectable citizens," said an article in Horizon Magazine in 1973, "for all of these settlements had in their structure a basic schizophrenia that, in time, would undo them – or at least alter them beyond recognition."

Even the promoters would come to realize that the real money was in long-term commercial growth and development, and would support the passing of laws and the hiring of marshals to enforce them.

But, to be sure, the triumph of civic values took some time. The cattle money was hard to give up; even the fines for violating the new ordinances were set to be easily within what a carousing cowboy or hard-working prostitute could afford to pay. Thus they weren't so much punishment as licensing fees and a new source of municipal income – for one town, $5,600 in a single season. "The revenue derived from fines on gambling and prostitution will pay the police force," its newspaper observed in 1879.

Over time, however, the respectable citizens prevailed. Town after town began truly insisting that guns be banned and whores be confined to their brothels, and even that drunks must be thrown in jail. By the end of the 1870s, towns were competing to be seen as the safest. Ellsworth claimed to be "the most orderly city. Here is order and law." In Wichita, a lawyer named S. M. Tucker grabbed his shotgun and led a vigilante group that faced down and jailed a Texas rustler named Hurricane Bill, who had been shooting up the town.

Dodge City held onto its reputation as a wild frontier town and a beacon for the cattle trade the longest. Founded in 1871 next to the Army's Fort Dodge on the Santa Fe Trail to New Mexico, its saloons first catered to off-duty soldiers from the fort. Then it became a shipping center for buffalo hides, and the customers were even less genteel buffalo hunters. In a single year during this period, twenty-four men were said to have been killed in Dodge City.

When the herds and their cowboys arrived, the saloon-keepers of Dodge had long understood the benefits of cut-rate volume business. They didn't boost drink prices for the thirsty cowhands. The town called itself the "cowboy capital of the world," proclaiming: "The grass is remarkably fine, the water plenty, drinks two for a quarter, and no grangers. These facts make Dodge City the cattle point."

Right up to the mid-1880s, Dodge kept its title as the wildest of the cow towns, with the prettiest women, the gaudiest dance halls, and the craziest cowboys. The town made gestures at law and order, including electing Bat Masterson as county sheriff and hiring Wyatt Earp as deputy marshal, but these sometime gunslingers caused about as much trouble as they cured.

Dodge City had perhaps its gaudiest moment near the end of its cow town career, in 1884. The trail herds were already thinning, and many of the other cattle towns had closed for business. But Caldwell, to the east, was still trying to compete. Then Dodge's ingenious saloon-keeper, Alonzo Webster, dreamed up an ambitious scheme to attract big crowds for a Fourth of July celebration: The town would stage a bullfight, Spanish style. The spectacle was expected to eclipse anything Caldwell could offer and lure hundreds of cattle shippers.

Webster talked the town's businessmen into

ponying up $10,000 for expenses, and built a crude bull ring. He found twelve actual longhorn bulls among all the steers and cows awaiting shipment, making sure they were more than ordinarily ornery. And he hired four genuine Mexican toreros and a picador, to whom he made the promise that at least one bull would be "fought to the death," without specifying whose death was involved.

Press coverage was divided, with some papers seeing this as a spectacular event, and others as a cruel, degrading spectacle. But hardly any ignored it. The bullfight was news even in faraway New York, where the *Herald* predicted that at least some of the matadors would be killed. For the promoters, the controversy was all the better for drumming up crowds.

When the day came, so did 4,000 spectators – three times the town's population – many of whom arrived by train. Those on horseback found all the town hitching posts occupied, and had to tether their horses to pickets in vacant fields.

The bullfight itself seems to have been a success. The first bull, a monstrous red specimen, put on a splendid show against the chief torero, Gregorio Gallardo, before the animal tired and was led from the ring. The next four bulls were far tamer, drawing hoots and catcalls from the bored crowd. So, for the day's finale, the red bull was called back, and again put up a good fight. Several times,

Gallardo only narrowly dodged his horns; once, he was pinned against a gate, suffering two broken ribs. But he slithered free and in the end, Gallardo killed the bull, using a Toledo sword said to be 150 years old. The crowd went away happy.

The newspaper in a nearby town, the *Larned Optic*, wrote about the spectacle: "Quite a number of our boys visited Dodge last week to see the bullfight. Some of them returned looking as though they had a personal encounter with the animals." But the damage wasn't done in the bullring. One man didn't get home at all; he was killed by a gambler in a shootout at Alonzo Webster's saloon.

That was Dodge City's last hurrah, and the beginning of the end for all the remaining cattle towns. The country was now far too thickly settled to tolerate cattle drives; and in 1885, the Kansas legislature passed a new, tough quarantine law banning Texas cattle from the entire state. This time the law was enforced, and by the end of that year, the trails were blocked at the border with barbed-wire fences. And finally, with no alternative, the cattlemen began paying the high cost of shipping cattle all the way from Texas.

EPILOGUE

The cow towns were history.

So was the heyday of the cowboy that the towns had enabled and embellished.

With the vanishing of the saloons, the desperadoes, the gamblers, the women, and the payoff sprees at the end of the long trail, the romantic figure of cowboy dwindled to what most cowboys had been all along – hard-working, tough, laconic outdoorsmen who endured endless hardships for far too little pay.

An evocation of the cowboy myth endured in the traveling spectacles that toured America and Europe for decades after the real show had folded. The most famous was William F. "Buffalo Bill" Cody's

Wild West Show, which perpetuated the cowboy legend for thirty years starting in 1883. Audiences were treated to horse races, sharpshooting feats, famous Indian chiefs, roping and riding displays, simulated buffalo hunts, bronco busting and the riding of untamed steers and buffalo - even a staged Indian attack on a settler's cabin, which ended with a rescue by cowboys toting six-guns.

Those shows were still touring as late as 1940, headlined by performers including Gene Autry and Tom Mix. And the myth lives on in the far tamer modern rodeo, in Hollywood movies, and in dude ranches sprinkled across the Western states. For many Americans still, the cowboy image is part of what they aspire to be: tough, independent, dependable and honorable - free spirits, but with an inner compass.

Real cowboys have lasted, too, still living the ethos of life on the Plains – tending cattle, mending fences, basking in the beauty of nature and enduring its fury. For most of them, pickup trucks have displaced ponies, and six-guns live mostly in bureau drawers, but they still share the mystique of the cowboy. The life isn't what it used to be, but then, it never was.

SOURCES

E. C. Abbott and Helena Huntington Smith, *We Pointed Them to the North: Recollections of a Cowpuncher* (Norman, Oklahoma: University of Oklahoma, 1966).

Andy Adams, T*he Log of a Cowboy: A Narrative of the Old Trial Days* (Lincoln, Nebraska: University of Nebraska, 1964).

Ramon F. Adams, *Come an' Get It: Story of the ld Cowboy Cook* (Norman, Oklahoma: University of Oklahoma, 1953).

Roman F. Adams, *The Old-Time Cowhand* (New York, New York: MacMillan, 1961).

Oren Arnold and John P. Hale, *Hot Irons: Heraldry*

of the Range (New York, New York: MacMillian, 1940).

Lewis Atherton, *The Cattle Kings* (Bloomington, Indiana: Indiana University, 1961).

James S. Brisbin, *The Beef Bonanza* (Norman, Oklahoma: University of Oklahoma, 1959).

Mark Brown and W. R. Felton, *Before Barbed Wire* (New York, New York: Bramhall, 1956).

John Clay, *My Life on the Range* (Norman, Oklahoma: University of Oklahoma, 1962).

Edward E. Dale, *The Range Cattle Industry: Ranching on the Great Plains from 1865 to 1925* (Norman, Oklahoma: University of Oklahoma Press, 1969).

J. Frank Dobie, *A Vaquero of the Brush Country* (Boston, Massachusetts: Little, Brown, 1960).

Harry Sinclair Drago, *Great American Cattle Trails* (New York, New York: Bramhall, 1965).

Cordia Sloan Duke and Joe B. Frantz, *6,000 Miles of Fence: Life on the XIT Ranch of Texas* (Austin, Texas: University of Texas, 1961).

Robert R. Dykstra, *The Cattle Towns* (New York, New York: Knopf, 1968).

J. B. Edwards, "Early Days in Abilene," *Abilene Daily Chronicle*, 1938.

Chris Emmett, *Shanghai Pierce: A Fair Likeness* (Norman, Oklahoma: University of Oklahoma, 1952).

Baylis John Fletcher, *Up the Trail in 79* (Norman, Oklahoma: University of Oklahoma, 1968).

Joe B. Franz and Julian E. Choate Jr., *The American Cowboy: The Myth and the Reality* (Norman, Oklahoma: University of Oklahoma, 1968).

Maurice Frink, *Cow Country Cavalcade: Eighty Years of the Wyoming Stock Growers Association* (Denver, Colorado: Old West, 1954).

Maurice Frink, W. Turrentine Jackson, and Agnes Wright Spring, *When Grass Was King* (Boulder, Colorado: University of Colorado, 1956.

Wayne Gard, *The Chisholm Trail* (Norman, Oklahoma: University of Oklahoma, 1969).

Wayne Gard, *Frontier Justice* (Norman, Oklahoma: University of Oklahoma, 1971).

J. Evetts Haley, *Charles Goodnight: Cowman and Plainsman* (Norman, Oklahoma: University of Oklahoma, 1970).

J. Evetts Haley, *The XIT Ranch of Texas and the Early Days of the Llano Estacado* (Norman, Oklahoma: University of Oklahoma, 1967).

Stuart Henry, *Conquering Our Great American Plains* (New York, New York: Dutton, 1930).

Emerson Hough, *The Story of the Cowboy* (Upper Saddle River, New Jersey: Gregg Press, 1970).

Joseph G. McCoy, *Historical Sketches of the Cattle Trade of the West and Southwest* (Austin, Texas: Arthur H. Clark, 1940).

A. S. Mercer, *The Banditti of the Plains* (Norman, Oklahoma: University of Oklahoma, 1968).

H. Nyle Miller and Joseph W. Snell, *Great Gunfighters of the Kansas Cowtowns* (Lincoln, Nebraska: University of Nebraska, 1967).

Ross Harmon Mothershead, *The Swan Land and Cattle Company Ltd.* (Norman, Oklahoma: University of Oklahoma, 1971).

Ernest S. Osgood, *The Day of the Cattleman* (Chicago, Illinois: University of Chicago, 1929).

Charles A. Siringo, *A Texas Cowboy or Fifteen Years on the Hurricane Deck of a Spanish Pony* (Lincoln, Nebraska: University of Nebraska, 1966).

John D. Smith, *The Wild West* (New York, New York: Doubleday, 1894).

Granville Stuart, *Forty Years on the Frontier* (Austin, Texas: Arthur H. Clark, 1967).

Stanley Vestal, *Queen of Cowtowns: Dodge City* (New York, New York: Harper, 1952).

Baron Walter Von Richthofen, *Cattle-Raising on*

the Plains of North American (Norman, Oklahoma: University of Oklahoma, 1969).

Walter Prescott Webb, *The Great Plains* (Grosset and Dunlap, 1957).

Manfred R. Wolfenstine, *The Manual of Brands and Marks* (Norman, Oklahoma: University of Oklahoma, 1970).

Chairwoman, CEO, and Publisher
Donna Carpenter LeBaron

Chief Financial Officer
Cindy Butler Sammons

Managing Editors
Molly Jones and C. David Sammons

Art Director
Matthew Pollock

Senior Editors
Hank Gilman, Ronald Henkoff, Ruth Hlavacek, Paul Keegan, Larry Martz, Ken Otterbourg

Associate Editors
Betty Bruner, Sherrie Moran, Val Pendergrast, Susan Peyton

President Emeritus
Helen Rees

Chairwoman Emeritus
Juanita C. Sammons

Made in the USA
Coppell, TX
09 December 2019